Venis Does Adonis while Apollo Shags a Tree

First Edition

Published by The Nazca Plains Corporation
Las Vegas, Nevada
2008

ISBN: 978-1-934625-67-5

Published by

The Nazca Plains Corporation ®
4640 Paradise Rd, Suite 141
Las Vegas NV 89109-8000

PUBLISHER'S NOTE
Venus Does Adonis while Apollo Shags a Tree is a work of fiction created wholly by *Tim Desmondes'* imagination. All characters are fictional and any resemblance to any persons living or deceased is purely by accident. No portion of this book reflects any real person or events.

Cover Images, Jenny Üksik and Cesco
Art Director, Blake Stephens

DEDICATION

This book is dedicated to all the gods who continue to live even though forsaken by mere mortals.

You gods shift shape to fit the flow of human history, but you never die.

So here's to you, Apollo and Venus, Isis and Osiris, Wotan and Brunhilde, and all the gods and goddesses who have been worshipped by our species since the dawn of consciousness.

You will exist long after humankind has become extinct.

First Edition

Tim Desmondes

TABLE OF CONTENTS

CHAPTER ONE   **9**
DAPHNE – THE VIRGIN LAUREL

CHAPTER TWO   **15**
IO SAYS MOO

CHAPTER THREE   **21**
CALLISTO GOES BEAR

CHAPTER FOUR   **27**
EUROPA AND THE BULL

CHAPTER FIVE   **31**
SEMELE ASKS A BOON

CHAPTER SIX   **39**
NARCISSUS AND ECHO

CHAPTER SEVEN   **43**
PYRAMUS, THISBE, AND THE HOLE IN THE WALL

CHAPTER EIGHT   **49**
VENUS GETS PROPOSALS

CHAPTER NINE   **53**
APOLLO GETS REJECTED

CHAPTER TEN   **57**
VENUS DOES OLYMPUS

CHAPTER ELEVEN   **65**
THE REVENGE OF VULCAN AND APOLLO

CHAPTER TWELVE   **69**
VENUS AND ADONIS

CHAPTER THIRTEEN   **75**

SAMACIS AND HERMAPHRODITUS

CHAPTER FOURTEEN 79
PLUTO PLEASURES PROSERPINE

CHAPTER FIFTEEN 85
CUPID'S PSYCHE GETS SHAGGED

CHAPTER SIXTEEN 91
A POET'S FOOTNOTE

CHAPTER SEVENTEEN 93
PASIPHAE GETS SHAGGED BY A BULL

CHAPTER EIGHTEEN 99
THESEUS: CAD, LOVER, PAL

CHAPTER NINETEEN 105
ARIADNE GOES WILD

CHAPTER TWENTY 111
ORPHEUS GOES TO HELL

CHAPTER TWENTY-ONE 117
PYGMALION SHAGS A STATUE

CHAPTER TWENTY-TWO 121
PERSEUS GIVES A FLYING SHAG

CHAPTER TWENTY-THREE 125
JASON, HERCULES, AND THE CATAMITE

CHAPTER TWENTY-FOUR 131
JASON SHAGS MEDEA

CHAPTER TWENTY-FIVE 137
JASON AND THE EVIL GODDESS

CHAPTER TWENTY-SIX 141
JASON THROWS THE BULL

CHAPTER TWENTY-SEVEN 143
SEXUAL FRUSTRATION ABOARD THE ARGO

CHAPTER TWENTY-EIGHT 149
HERCULES: STRONGMAN/TRANSVESTITE

CHAPTER TWENTY-NINE 155
ATALANTA FALLS FOR AN APPLE

CHAPTER THIRTY 161
CEPHALUS SHOOTS THE BREEZE

CHAPTER THIRTY-ONE 165
GLAUCUS SHAGS A MERMAID

ABOUT THE AUTHOR 171

CHAPTER I

DAPHNE – THE VIRGIN LAUREL

Apollo had fooled around a lot before he caught his first glimpse of Daphne. But with that first sighting, he fell madly in love. The electric currents that burst through his scrotum were ignited by both love and lust. Lust alone had sent a delightful current to his gonads heretofore. But this new additional feeling produced an erection like nothing he had previously experienced.

I'll tell you how this situation came about.

Daphne was a nymph, nearly divine, being the daughter of Peneus, the river-god.

When Apollo caught sight of her, it was not blind lust that quickened his libido. It was the malicious mischievous prank of Cupid that instigated the love-struck phallic rising.

Apollo, who was a credible archer had caught sight of Cupid who was idly fluttering about, flexing his bowstring.

"Hey, you snot-nosed brat," grumbled Apollo. "What the hell do you think you're doing with weapons that should be wielded only by big, strong he-gods like me? Why don't you just content yourself with lighting little love-fires that will make mortal men horny and mortal women hotties, you little twerp?"

The tiny winged god did not take the sun god's taunt well.

He answered, "Shoot your arrows any fucking way you want, Goldilocks. You can take your potshots at mortal creatures 'til the cows come home. I am about to wing a god. So, small I may be, yet I am greater than you in the long run."

With that, the little imp fluttered his wings, rose up in the air, and landed on Mount Parnassus. He dug into his quiver and pulled out two arrows, arrows with opposite powers.

One of the arrows was golden, with a sharp gleaming point. It was the arrow that arouses love, lust, and amatory madness. The other arrow was blunt and lead tipped and quenches the mad passions of love.

The scamp fit the lead-tipped missile to his bowstring and shot it into the heart of Peneus' daughter. And quick as a flash, he shot the other arrow right into Apollo's ripe libido.

The nymph was aware of the horny god who was ogling her and took off into the woods. She now had no interest whatsoever in men or male gods. She went traipsing after the sylvan creatures with the mad abandon of Artemis, goddess of the hunt.

Daphne ran to her father for protection. But Peneus was far from sympathetic to her disdain of love.

"Father," she pleaded. "It's not enough that mortal men chase me with sex-crazed eyes. Now there's even a god who has the hots for me."

"Wonderful, wonderful, child," Peneus replied. "Like most mature creatures, I'd like a bunch of grandsons. Mortal little buggers would be fine. But if you could get laid by an Olympian, too, once in a while, that would be even better."

"Daddy, daddy," she cried. "I don't want to get laid at all. You're a demigod. You could grant me eternal virginity."

She put her arms around her father's neck.

"Please, Daddy. Please!"

How could the demigod refuse his lovely daughter's request? He yielded, although he could not help but regret that his favorite child would not give birth to heirs, be they mortal or immortal.

However the gift of virginity Peneus had granted to his daughter did nothing to mollify Apollo's phallus. The god stalked the nymph wherever she fled.

There was no aspect of the nymph that did not stir the god's ardor. Sweet talk had always worked for him before, and he couldn't believe it wasn't turning the trick for him now.

"You are *such* a doll," he enthused. "I love your hair, your eyes, your fingers..."

No soap!

"Slow down," he urged. "Lambs flee the wolf. Deer run from the lion. Doves fly away from the eagle. But I am not like the wolf, the lion, or the eagle. My pursuit is the pursuit of true love. Slow down and let's talk."

Daphne looked over her shoulder even as she kept up her brisk pace. The groin of the god was graced with an aroused member, betraying that the pursuer's words were hollow. To her, he *was* the wolf, the lion, the eagle.

He pleaded to her with honeyed tongue.

"I worry, fair nymph, that you will stumble and fall. You could bruise yourself, or worse, break one or both of your winsome legs. If you would only slow down, I promise I will too. Better yet, stop altogether and I'll do the same. Stop and ask me who I am. I'm not some loathsome mountain grill, no ignorant shepherd who smells like sheep-dip. If you would only let me tell you who I am you would give in. My father is Jupiter himself. I am Apollo, the god of music and of everything that is beautiful and wonderful. I discovered the art of medicine and healing herbs. But there is not an herb on this earth that can cure my lovesickness for you. Stop, damn it. I'm the handsomest creature in creation. Girls go wild about me. Just think of what you might be missing..."

While the god was both running and sweet-talking at the same time, he realized his words were being wasted on the empty air. Because Daphne was outrunning him.

As she distanced herself, the winds bared her legs and set her gown a-flutter. Her gorgeous hair streamed out in charming disarray.

Apollo's eyes and phallus were enchanted at the lovely sight.

He sped after her, urged on by hope, lust, and love. She picked up even greater speed urged on by fear.

At last, being a mere nymph and not a goddess, Daphne was overcome with fatigue. She spied a stream ahead and stopped to address the flowing water which was, of course, her father's domain.

"O Daddy, Daddy," she cried. "Help me. You promised me. You promised me. Take away my beauty that has brought me to this wretched situation."

The words were hardly out of her mouth when she felt a heaviness in her arms and legs. Her soft, warm skin began to change to bark. Her flowing hair transformed into leaves. Her arms became branches. Her gorgeous feet burrowed into the earth, becoming roots.

She was no longer a nymph, but she was still beautiful nonetheless.

Apollo was no stranger to metamorphoses, and loved Daphne in her new form. He placed his hand on her trunk and felt her heart still aflutter beneath the location where her breasts had been. He caressed the limbs and kissed the wood. He pressed his phallus into the crevice where her pudenda had been. And in an ecstasy, he made love to the laurel tree.

In his divine voice, he sang: "You cannot now be my sweetheart. But you shall forever be my tree. I shall wear a wreath of you in my hair forevermore. My lyre and my quiver will be bedecked with your wreath. Whenever an athlete or a general prevails, he will have a laurel wreath placed upon his brow."

When Apollo returned to the halls of Olympus, his fellow gods were laughing at his arrival.

"What's the big joke?" he asked.

When the laughter died down, Jupiter slapped him on the back.

"Well, Apollo," he chuckled. "All of us up here on Olympus were watching you fucking a tree. Funniest thing any of us had ever seen."

"You must be mistaken," quoth Apollo. "I was just there visiting the country."

Jupiter could never resist a good pun, and answered: "Right, Blue Eyes. And I'm sure you will visit the cunt-tree again and again."

The halls of Olympus rang with divine laughter at the joke of the king of the gods.

Apollo took no offense. He strummed his lyre and sang a love song addressed to his Daphne...his Cunt-tree.

The gods' laughter turned to tears as they realized that Apollo truly was still in love. And how sad it was that his love was a tree, and not a nymph.

CHAPTER II

IO SAYS MOO

Inachus, like Peneus, was a river deity. But unlike Peneus, he had fathered many daughters. And, although semi-divine, he was king of the realm of Argos.

Good King Inachus was shedding copious tears one fine summer day. For he could find no trace of his favorite daughter Io. He had sought her for days and discovered not a trace of the fair nymph. He feared that she might be nowhere, a fate worse than death. Were she in Hades, Inachus could bear knowing she was at least with the shades. But to be nowhere? An unbearable thought.

As a matter of fact, the fair Io was somewhere. She had some days previous emerged very physically from a softly flowing stream over which her father held rule.

Jupiter happened to be roaming the woods adjacent to the river in search of a bit of fornication. There were few gods or mortals more randy than the king of the gods.

Jupiter emerged from the woods and looked around, and seeing the luscious nymph emerging nude and dripping from the stream sprang an enormous erection.

Io, like so many of her sisters, was not adverse to a bit of sport in the woods and meadows. And the majesty of the phallus she spied at the groin of the powerful being she beheld caused a warm oozing from between her thighs.

"Good day, fair nymph," the god smiled. "It is a lovely afternoon for a romp in the woods. If you would deign to enter yonder copse, I would be honored to protect you from any danger."

Io feigned reluctance. A pure tease, of course.

"Look," Jupiter persisted. "I can assure you that you will be safe with me. I am not just any old creature, or a common god. I am the god who holds heaven's mighty scepter in his hand."

Io was very aware of the mighty scepter the divine character was caressing with his hand, and was quite intrigued.

She took his free hand in hers and willingly accompanied the horny god into the woods.

Never had the nymph met with sweeter dalliance than she experienced with the monarch of Olympus. He not only made magnificent love. He demonstrated that in amorous matters, size does, indeed, count.

While Jupiter and Io were frolicking in the woods, Juno glanced down from Olympus and her eye fell on the woods of Argos.

She was of a suspicious nature, and with good reason. Her husband, Jupiter, was an incurable philanderer. And she was on to him.

What aroused her suspicions was a dark cloud bank hovering over a wooded area there in Argos. She well knew what river mists and fogs looked like. This was something quite different. Something smelled fishy.

She looked around Olympus and through the skies to see if she could spot her husband. When he was not anyplace where he belonged, she had a good idea what was afoot.

Gentle reader. There is a message here for you if you read on. If the king of the gods could not get by with a bit of hanky-panky, how do you, a mere mortal, expect to get away with cheating on your spouse?

Juno glided down to earth, to Argos, and caused the suspicious cloud to evaporate.

Jupiter had created the cloud cover to deceive his wife while he disported himself with the delectable nymph. But, like many a husband, he kept his senses cocked for any possible conjugal interruption. Before his wife could catch him red-handed, he abruptly withdrew from the act and changed Io into a white heifer. And even as a cow, she was still a great fuck.

"All right, Jupiter," Juno snarled. "What's with the dark cloud that was hovering over you?"

"Cloud, cloud?" the god replied. "I don't see any cloud anywhere."

"That's because I dispelled it. That cloud was hiding some kind of monkey business."

"No monkey business going on here, Dear, I assure you," he countered.

"And that cow. What are you doing here with a white cow?"

"Cow?" the god asked, as though surprised. "What cow?"

"That cow, the white heifer that you have your back to," Juno pointed out.

"Oh, that cow. I was just admiring her. Lovely creature, isn't she?"

"All right, Jupiter," the wife snarled. "Where did this cow come from? Whose herd does she belong to?"

"You may find this hard to believe, my dear," Jupiter replied. "Uh, uh, uh...but you see..."

"Go on, Jupe," Juno urged. "What am I going to find hard to believe?"

"Well, as it so happens," the god stumbled, waiting for inspiration. "As it so happens, this beautiful heifer just sprang up here out of the earth. Amazing, isn't it?

"Incredible indeed, husband. Absolutely remarkable. I assume from what you say, then, that the beast does not belong to anyone's herd."

Jupiter conceded the point, wondering if his wife was setting some sort of trap for him.

"Then, my dear husband," she concluded. "There is no reason that you couldn't give her to me as a gift. I would just *love* that."

Jupiter gulped. He could scarcely give his newest lover to his wife. But not to do so would make Juno suspicious.

To give his lover to his wife (who, incidentally was also his sister) would be a despicable act. But not to do so would further Juno's suspicions and would certainly lead to marital disputes and discomfort.

There was no question. Tough luck for Io. But Jupiter just had to hand the cow over to Juno.

So Juno now owned Io. Which did not allay her suspicions. A constant eye had to be kept on the cow. Nay, not *an* eye. A hundred eyes.

So, when Jupiter beat a hasty retreat from the field, Juno took her cow to Argus to watch over her.

Argus was just the one to keep watch. He had a hundred eyes set around his head. Two of his eyes at a time closed in sleep, while ninety-eight stayed awake. So wherever he turned, he would be looking at Io.

In the daytime, Argus let Io graze freely. But at night he haltered her.

She grazed on grass and leaves and herbs. She slept on the hard cold ground and drank from muddy streams.

She tried to stretch her arms out to Argus in supplication, only to realize that she had no arms, only legs. She attempted to plead with him, but only ended up mooing. When she saw her reflection in the streams, her aspect frightened her.

Her nymph sisters who inhabited the streams did not recognize her.

Io's father Inachus emerged from his river and was able to recognize that his daughter, for whom he had been searching, had somehow metamorphosed into a cow. He spoke tender words to his Io, but received naught but moos for a reply.

Argus knew his job. His loyalty was all to Juno. So he drove Io away from her father's tender words to pastures far from the rivers ruled over by the demigod.

Meanwhile, Jupiter's lust for Io persisted. Nymphlike or cowlike, she was a terrific lay. He had to get her away from Argus.

So he called on his wily son, Mercury.

"Mercury, my beloved son," Jupiter exclaimed. "Your father is consumed with love sickness. I won't go into details, but you can help put me out of my agony."

"A bad case of lover's nuts, eh, Dad?", Mercury sympathized. "I'm here to help. Sounds like you have an adventure in store for me."

Jupiter gave his son a simple task. All Mercury had to do to help his father with his aching balls was fly down to earth and kill Argus.

"An interesting challenge," thought the messenger god. "Finding a way to dispatch a guy who always keeps ninety-eight eyes awake will call for a bit of sly skullduggery."

That was just Mercury's meat.

So he slipped on his winged sandals, put on his magic cap that made him invisible, and picked up his sleep-producing wand.

He flew down to earth, took off his cap, and set aside his wings. He did, however, keep his wand.

Disguised as a goatherd and rustling up a flock of goats as he traversed the countryside, he approached Argus. When he got within earshot of the hundred-eyed one, he played his reed pipe.

Argus, who had an ear for music, called out to the goatherd.

"Yo, goatherd musician. Come on over here and join me. The pasture is lush with grass. I've got a nice shady spot here. Your goats can graze alongside the heifer I'm watching over."

Mercury could keep anyone entertained with his stories, his lies, and his music.

As he spun his tales and piped his tunes, Argus' eyes grew sleepier and sleepier. First two eyes yielded to slumber. Then four. And so on up to ninety-eight. When the final pair of eyes yielded, Mercury waved his sleep-inducing wand over his companion to deepen the sleep to a deep, deep slumber.

When he was sure no eye would be able to peek, Mercury drew his hooked sword and beheaded Juno's watchdog.

Argus' head with its hundred eyes rolled in a bloody mess down the hill on which he and Mercury had been keeping company.

Juno immediately became aware that her watchman had been dispatched. She descended to earth and, first, gathered up Argus' eyes and set them on the tail of her bird, the peacock. The bird's tail now was beset with star-like jewels.

Juno sent a gadfly to torment her heifer rival. The poor beast was driven from Greece, traversed the Levant, and finally entered Egypt. On the banks of the Nile, she prostrated herself, raised her head heavenward, and with mooings Jupiter could hear and understand, besought his succor.

Jupiter had to intervene. As a nymph or as a cow, she was a great fuck. He confessed his infidelity to his wife and asked her forgiveness. He promised to give up Io if Juno would send away the gadfly and let Io resume her former shape.

Io resumed her nymph form. Her moos became words. And, best yet, the Egyptians, astounded by the transformation from cow to nymph, took her to be a goddess. And thereby, fair nymphs and maidens, here lies a message. If you would hope to metamorphose into a goddess, it might be a good idea to give in to the amorous advances of any god who propositions you. Particularly if he is well-hung. He might be able to advance your career. Being an Egyptian goddess is not a bad gig.

CHAPTER III

CALLISTO GOES BEAR

Just because Jupiter gave up Io, it did not follow that he gave up chasing nymphs. God that he was, he was no wiser than mortal husbands. He simply could not disabuse himself of the myth that husbands can get by with infidelities.

The king of the gods felt that the only way he could console himself for the loss of Io was to cruise the earth's meadows, vales, woods, and glades. With a modest expenditure of persistence, a toothsome, willing nymph was sure to be encountered somewhere.

As he was trolling for action in Arcadia, mooning still a bit for Io, he heard a dulcet sound. It was a hum, and from its tone, it was clear that it was being emitted by a female.

Jupiter peeked from around a tree and spied a lovely grassy glade that banked a gently flowing stream. But it was not the glade or the stream that engaged his attention. For lying languidly on the lawn was the source of the music. And that source was a lovely naked nymph humming a gentle tune to herself.

As she hummed her merry melody, her graceful left hand was entertaining her shapely breast whilst her right hand caressed her pussy. The sight caused his heart to quicken and his libido to throb.

As he further surveyed the area adjacent to the nymph, he spied a bow and a quiver full of arrows.

The situation called for a strategy. The nymph was clearly a votary of Diana the huntress, the moon goddess.

Diana was one of Jupiter's daughters, a product, like her brother Apollo, of Jupiter's flirtation with Latona. Unlike her brother Apollo, Diana was not into omnisexual promiscuity. She was a virgin and her sexual outlet was through lesbian and autoerotic activities.

Like her brother, she was also skilled with bow and arrow and pursued the hunt assiduously.

All the members of Diana's coterie had to have similar characteristics. First and foremost, all were virginae intactae. In addition to possessing unbroken hymens, the female had to own bow and arrows and to fell deer on the run with the weapon. Beyond those qualifications, an active inclination towards members of their own sex and a proclivity towards creative masturbation were required qualities.

The nymph Jupiter was ogling was in high favor with his chaste daughter Diana. The god was not aware of that, but had he known it, it would not have dampened his lusty enthusiasm. If there was any conquest he enjoyed more than any other, it was the joy of freeing a maiden from her virginity.

"This one is for me," thought the wily god. "It's unlikely that Juno will be spying on Arcadia. But it would be worth it even if she were to catch me in flagrante delicto. I'm willing to withstand her bitchiness for what will surely be a grand fuck."

He knew that the nymph would be turned off by the approach of a male being. Even more-so by a male hung as lavishly as himself. So he changed himself into the very likeness of his daughter Diana. He grew a voluptuous pair of breasts. His legs assumed the shapeliness of a ballerina. But the greatest change occurred to the organs that nestled between his legs. He now had a hot cunt.

In the guise, then, of Diana, Jupiter approached Callisto in splendid nudity.

Callisto continued to play her fingers teasingly over her moist cunt.

"Welcome, dear goddess," she cooed. "O goddess more awesome and powerful than Jupiter himself."

Jupiter laughed at the thought that he was prized higher than himself. To him the irony of the statement was a source of great amusement.

Jupiter lay down beside Callisto and replaced his hands on the areas where she had been enjoying herself. His touch on her breasts was so light and grazing that her lips emitted a series of delighted yelps. His other hand that explored the elfin forest of curly hair on her mons veneris slipped gradually down to her moist fragrant twat.

As the fingers of that hand became bathed in the elixir the nymph was discharging from her vagina, his middle finger probed the entrance to her divine sheath. Bit by bit, massaging the vagina with skillful amorous pulsations, he reached the intact hymen. Ah, yes. The goal had been established.

While the god was thus exciting the nymph to a frenzy, he leaned over and kissed first her forehead, then her cheeks, and then her lips. As his lips pressed against hers, her hands were playfully tracing his newly emerged female bosom. As he perceived one of her hands caressing his ass, he inserted his tongue into her mouth and engaged in a playful duel of tongue with tongue.

Jupiter rolled his body atop hers, and felt a transformation in the female body he was wearing. The breasts receded to their former manly form. His female labia extended downward to form a scrotum that contained his panting nuts. And his clitoris sprang forth into the mighty hardon of the god who ruled heaven and earth.

As his finger withdrew from the lovely orifice, it was replaced by the powerful scepter of the wielder of thunderbolts.

With a gasp, as the mighty phallus drove through the virginal hymen, Callisto realized that it was not Diana who was making love to her. She had been somehow betrayed. She had been violated.

And as the life force of her companion filed her womb, she felt exhilaration, bafflement, and deep sorrow.

Satisfied that he had eluded his wife's apprehension of his conquest, Jupiter kissed Callisto on the forehead and departed the scene for Olympus' heights.

Callisto had always loved the woods and forests in which she hunted. Now, in her shame, she detested them for having witnessed her ravishment and knowing her shameful secret. She gathered up her bow and arrows and began to walk away from the lea upon which she had been robbed of her treasure.

But lo! Descending the slopes of Mount Maenalus, and accompanied by her train of virginal nymphs, is the goddess Diana herself. The troop is in high good spirits, rejoicing in the success of the hunt.

Diana called out to Callisto in joyous greeting. But, at first, Callisto fled, fearing that this was Jupiter returning again in disguise. But when she realized that such could not be the case, since the other nymphs were accompanying her, Callisto turned about and joined the band.

Callisto felt pangs of great guilt. She feared that her loss of virginity might somehow be revealed in her face, her walk, or her general demeanor. But the goddess and the other virgin nymphs could not detect Callisto's change of status.

It has been rumored, however, that three of the nymphs did detect Callisto's condition. Which arouses suspicion that these three had also secretly experienced coital engagements. But rumors from Arcadia hopefully remain in Arcadia.

As month followed month, the seed planted by Jupiter in Callisto's womb unfolded into a fetus. The swelling of the belly bellied the cloak of chastity worn by the nymph. Of all the band, it was Diana who espied the evidence of pregnancy last.

And in the harshest of tones, Diana dismissed Callisto from her band.

As the queen of the heavens and earth, Juno had myriad sources of information. And by a confluence of spies, she had acquired intelligence that the nymph Callisto was carrying Jupiter's seed. But she did not plan to wreak her vengeance on the nymph immediately. There would be a fitting time for that. So Juno waited.

In due time Callisto gave birth to a son, whom she named Arcas.

It was the birth of Arcas that sent Juno's ire over the top.

She descended to Arcadia and appeared before the terrified young mother.

"So, Slut," she rasped. "I see that your adultery has produced a son. And now, as the boy goes through life, his very existence will broadcast how I've been wronged and how sloppy my husband is in his sordid little escapades.

"You are going to suffer, Girl. That precious beauty of yours by which you provoked my husband's lust... It's history."

With those spiteful words, the goddess grabbed Callisto by the hair and flung her down to the ground.

Callisto strove to stretch out her arms to the goddess in supplication. And to her horror, she saw those arms growing shaggy hair. Her arms morphed into feet and her hands into sharp-clawed paws. Her mouth and jaws transformed themselves into maws. Her voice, which she sought to use to implore mercy became a deep growl. Juno had metamorphosed the nymph into a bear. But a bear with human feelings.

Having spent her spite, Juno returned to Olympus. Callisto was left to roam the woods of Arcadia, pursued by hounds, hunters, and preying wild beasts.

Thus Callisto lived for eighteen years in constant terror. Her son Arcas grew up to be a hunter, with not a clue to the curse Juno had exercised on his mother.

Finally, the inevitable occurred. While out a-hunting, Arcas came upon his mother. With a mother's sensibilities, Callisto recognized her son. But Arcas had no way of knowing the bear was his own mother.

He took clear aim at the bear's breast with his lethal spear.

Jupiter became aware of the impending tragedy even as the youth was taking aim. And Jupiter stayed the youth's hand and sent a whirlwind into Arcadia that encircled mother and son and transported them to the heavens above Olympus. And there he gave Arcas the form of a bear.

In the northern skies, the two bears dance and give guidance to wanderers and seamen and inspiration to poets.

When dark clouds veil the heavens even from the eyes of the Olympians, Jupiter dares to rise above the clouds to visit Callisto. She is content to entertain the god in her heavenly abode. And Jupiter had, and has, no aversion to engaging in the fucking with a bear, nor, indeed, with any kind of creature whatsoever.

And what of Arcas?

Under similar cover of clouds, Venus and her followers and playmates, the Nereid's, soar up to the heavens to engage in a fuck fest with Arcas. For though Venus' voluptuaries are seldom into bestiality, sexual activities with Arcas, since he had been born of a nymph and fathered by a god, was an exception.

Thus, on evenings when a layer of clouds veils the heavens above, it is likely that it is party time in the northern skies.

CHAPTER IV

EUROPA AND THE BULL

At the eastern end of the Mediterranean Sea, the city of Tyre was founded by Agenor. And around that city, he established his kingdom of Sidon eons before the Phoenicians conquered the area and made Sidon and Tyre their own.

Agenor sired five sons and one daughter. His daughter was the princess Europa.

From the time she was quite young, she was a phallophile. She was simply fascinated by the pricks of all the males in the kingdom.

When she grew into maturity, her fascination became an obsession. She gave a great deal of attention to the area of her own body that lacked a cock and balls. Not that she scorned the lovely breasts she had grown. She frequently fondled them with pleasure. And she was quite fond of the pleasure she experienced when she caressed her cunt and clit. And her delight was complete when she ran a slim white finger into her receptive vagina.

Since it was the habit of the citizens of Tyre to spurn the encumbrance of clothing, she was able to make judgments on the quality of the endowments of the young men of the kingdom.

During the course of her entire eighteenth year, she had experienced the gratification of having been penetrated by the pricks of no less than one thousand youths.

Alas! None satisfied. Some were too short. Others too thin. Still others too flaccid. And so forth and so on.

What the damsel craved was penetration by a truly satisfying giant dong.

Up on Olympus, Jupiter became aware of the plight of the Asiatic princess, and out of deep compassion he desired to intervene.

To this end, he summoned his messenger, Mercury, to his side.

"Welcome, Son," Jupiter greeted the messenger god. "I have a little task I'd like you to perform for me."

Now Mercury was possibly the wiliest of the gods. He had figured out very early that to be in daddy's good graces was highly beneficial. He often reminded himself that "when you're good to Daddy, Daddy's good to you."

"Sure, Dad," the wing-sandaled god replied. "Anything you say, I'll get it done."

Jupiter didn't tell his son the reason for the task he was about to commission. He didn't need to. The commissions of the king of the gods nearly always had concupiscent motives underpinning them.

"Good boy. I want you to fly on down to earth to the land that looks up at your mother's star from the left. It is called the Kingdom of Sidon. You will spy a herd of cattle there that belongs to the king. It will be grazing on a mountainside some distance from the seashore. I want you to drive that herd down to the shore of the beach."

No sooner had the words escaped Jupiter's mouth than Mercury landed in Sidon and drove the herd right down to the shore where Europa was playing stoop tag with her Tyrian playmates.

As the herd was moving among the lovely young ladies, Jupiter took on the form of a bull and appeared suddenly in the herd. He lowed much like the others. He looked much like the others. Except that he was far more beautiful to the earthly eye than any other bull.

28

He was snowy white. The muscles of his neck were beautifully rounded. A long dewlap hung down in front and an awesome pair of balls descended from the rear. His horns were twisted in shapes of artistic excellence. And his eyes! They held an expression of great contentment, but also of yearning.

Europa spotted the gorgeous bull and was strongly attracted to him. Such a handsome, friendly appearing beast. She gathered a bouquet of posies and extended them towards the taurine marvel.

The bull felt the tingle of love way down into his giant balls. He skillfully kissed her lily-white hands. He gamboled sportively about before her, then laid down on the sands of the beach, gazing up at her with winsome devotion.

Europa approached, patted his gorgeous pelt, and, retrieving additional flowers, created garlands to encircle his horns.

She bade him arise, which he did with such grace as never before was beheld in the bovine species.

Europa felt that at last she had met a lover who could satisfy the needs of her yearning love chamber.

First she examined the enticing scrotum of her bull. Magnificent. She had to run her tongue over the sack and kiss every inch.

She had to see the pizzle extend to display its magnitude. The kissing of the twin orbs had initiated the desired action.

When the bull's grand organ emerged to full hard state, Europa knew that her wishes and hopes could be fulfilled by the magnificent beast. For Europa, size mattered. But not there on the beach with her coterie of young ladies observing.

Jupiter, in his bull's guise, knelt down so the princess could heist herself onto his back. She leaned forward and whispered into his ear.

"O magnificent and well-hung beast. Thou art indeed magnificent. I would that you satisfy my long-held dream. If thou canst understand human speech, I beseech thee, take me away from the sight of my companions that we may fuck in private and that I may take thee as my lover."

With a soft lowing sound, the bull revealed that he understood the invitation to engage in exquisite lovemaking.

He marched to the shore with his lover seated proudly on his back. He entered the sea and set out for the island of Crete.

Europa waved back at the Asian shore she knew she would never see again.

The god transported his lover to the romantic isle, where he made savage, beautiful love to her. She returned his ardor, and, for the first time in her life was truly filled and fulfilled.

The people of Crete worshipped Jupiter in his form of a bull. Elatus, the youthful king of Crete, took Europa to wife.

Europa gave birth to twin sons, gifts of the seed of Jupiter. The boys were named Minos and Rhadamantus, who later became Judges of the Dead.

And, of course, Europa will be forever remembered as the princess who gave her name to the continent of Europe.

CHAPTER V

SEMELE ASKS A BOON

When Europa was whisked away from Tyre, King Agenor was perplexed and aggrieved. He sent his five sons out into the world to locate their sister in order to return her to the kingdom.

His son Cadmus traveled south and then west, arriving in the city of Thebes in Egypt. He did not find his sister there, but during his sojourn in Thebes he became acquainted with an early form of hieroglyphics. From that base he invented a sixteen letter alphabet that was the first trial for what later became the Greek alphabet.

Still searching for his sister Europa, he sailed across the sea and arrived in Greece. He founded a city there in Thrace which he named Thebes in memory of the Egyptian metropolis that had intrigued him so.

Cadmus finally gave up his quest for his sister and settled down in his newly founded city. He married and fathered six children. The fairest of the six he named Semele.

Semele was every bit as beautiful as her Aunt Europa. And beauty like that could not fail to catch the eye of Jupiter.

The king of the gods escaped from Juno's surveillance over him, and he came to Semele's villa as a suitor of sorts.

Semele, unlike her aunt, did not need an enormous dick to satisfy her. Jupiter, then, used a more conventional approach than taking on the form of a bull. He seduced her with flattery, gifts, sweet talk, and empty promises.

Semele had had lovers before Jupiter. But none had the panoply of seductive tactics of the god.

She desired to know exactly who her new lover was, but Jupiter was reluctant to tell her.

At length, the sweet young thing, who was able to give as well as receive, had Jupiter thoroughly entranced. He soon felt that he absolutely must have her loving.

One evening, he arrived in Thebes at a time when his nuts ached for need of loving. Semele admitted him, allowed him to engage in divine foreplay, and when he was aroused to a delicious painful degree, refused to allow his entrance to her treasure chest unless he told her who he was.

There is not a male, be he mortal or god, who can withstand a female demand when his balls are in an uproar. Jupiter relented and told her the truth. Semele gave in and Jupiter enjoyed an evening in her bed that was truly memorable.

The result of that engagement was a pregnancy. For Semele was fertile and Jupiter's seed was potent.

And, as always, Juno's sources informed her of what had transpired.

Juno was furious. So angry that she had to transfer her feelings from Europa to Semele. What was it, she wondered, about Agenor's family that continued to cause her so much embarrassment.

"A lot of good it does me to be angry at Jupiter. He's not the laughing stock. I am," Juno complained. "It's bad enough that he's shagging every nymph and Nereid down below. He has to knock them up as well. And now it's mortal princesses and who knows what else. If he could just engage his baton in trees like my stepson Apollo, everyone wouldn't be laughing at me."

On and on the goddess raged. She was determined to get her revenge. Semele would have to pay.

Juno wrapped herself in a saffron colored cloud and descended to Thrace. She assumed the disguise of an old woman, turning her hair white, wrinkling her skin, and walking all stooped over. She hobbled about, and, at last, looked, spoke, and walked exactly like Beroe, Semele's old nurse.

Semele was delighted with the visit from the person she recognized as Beroe. The two sat down for a royal old gossip fest. Juno knew all about the matters that the princess and the aged nurse usually discussed. In time the goddess brought up mention of Jupiter's name.

Semele admitted that she was engaged in a torrid affair with the god.

"With Jupiter, you say," the crone sighed. "I just hope you are right. But many a young lady has been deceived along those lines you know."

Semele asked her how.

"Why there are many young scamps who become involved with attractive girls. They pretend to be gods and the maidens yield favors to them, lured by the excitement that they are having an affair with real Olympians.

"Oh, the things they do! Whatever the villain wants her to do, she goes ahead and pleases him. Before you know it, he gets her pregnant and then goes off to some other part of the country to seduce the next girl who catches his eye. Oh, my dear. You just cannot be too careful."

It was hard for Semele to believe that any mere mortal could make love as exquisitely as her lover. And yet...?

"I really believe my lover is Jupiter," she said, with some hesitation showing in her voice.

"Why don't you find out for sure?" the crone asked. "Make him prove that he's Jupiter."

"How could I do that?" asked Semele.

"Easy, my dear. Easy," the supposed nurse answered. "Next time he comes, tease him up to the point where he is so stimulated that his prick is quivering and he must have sexual release or burst. Tell him that you will not spread your legs for him unless he will grant you a boon.

"He will be so worked up he cannot deny you anything. Then, when he agrees, tell him to show himself to you in all his godly glory. Then, if your lover really is Jupiter, he will have to appear to you in his shiny splendor. You will be one of the few mortals ever to have seen the king of the gods in the guise the Olympians see him in. The exquisite goddess Juno sees him in his glory all the time. Why shouldn't you?

"Surprise him by making him swear to grant the boon when he's red hot. If he truly is Jupiter, the pleasure of having the divine baton enter your treasured duct will certainly be the most glorious sexual experience any mortal woman could imagine."

Semele was intrigued by the idea and told her companion she would follow through.

Juno cackled as a hag would. But her wifely heart rejoiced that her revenge would be plied on the guileless mortal.

That very evening Jupiter came calling at Semele's villa. He was definitely ready for action and could hardly wait for her to open the door in response to his knock.

Semele opened the door and smiled her most seductive smile.

She had put in some fine Samian wine which she served up to her godlike swain. Jupiter drank down the inebriating delicacy and urged his new sweetheart to match him goblet for goblet. Semele, however, managed to adulter her portions sufficiently to keep sober enough to carry out her plan.

When it was clear that Jupiter was in an advanced mood for love, she invited him to join her in the boudoir.

She slowly removed his skimpy garb from the magnificent torso and divested herself of her gown, making sure that her lovely features peeked at the god in tantalizing glimpses.

Jupiter stretched out on the bed, showing his anticipation with a massive hardon.

Semele then proceeded to show herself the seductress rather than the one seduced. She plied every manner that raises a male to the height of frenzy.

She kissed her lover on the mouth with ardor. Then she proceeded to kiss every inch of his bare body while fondling his varied erogenous zones. She then licked her tongue over the areas where he showed himself most stimulated, giving full attention to every fold and crevice. She inserted her tongue into every orifice that could give entry to that organ. She arranged herself so that the god's lips had full access to her own most private areas.

When Jupiter's body demanded release, he told the princess to grant him access to her treasure trove.

"Yes, Love," she agreed. "I am ready for your attentions. But first, will you promise me that you will grant me a boon?"

"Yes, yes!" Jupiter panted.

"Anything I want?" Semele persisted.

The wait was driving Jupiter to near madness.

"Yes, yes, Dear. Just name it. You can have it. Now give me access to that sweet damp garden of delights that dwells between your legs."

"You really swear to that?" she demanded.

"Yes, yes, damn it," he fairly shouted, close to madness in his intense desire. "I swear by the River Styx."

That is the oath which is absolutely unbreakable by all the gods of Olympus.

"Very well then, my love," Semele smiled. "You may enter me however you will. But you must reveal yourself to me in all your glory. I would see you as Juno sees you when you show yourself to her when you are ready to make love."

Jupiter emitted a doleful cry. He could not break his oath.

He rapidly ascended Mount Olympus. He clothed himself in his full godly magnificence. He returned immediately to Thrace, though with reluctance. He entered the villa.

When Semele observed the god clothed in all his glory, she was consumed and perished on the spot. However, she gave premature birth to the child in her womb.

Jupiter saved the child and sewed him up in his thigh. There the child, Bacchus, grew to full term maturity and erupted into the world to become the god of wine, revelry, and the joys of sensuality.

Jupiter's despondency over the loss of Semele was partially mitigated by the saving of his son.

Her vengeance complete, Juno forgave her husband, and they were able to enjoy one another's company and pleasant conversation again.

One day, when Jupiter and Juno had imbibed bountiful portions of wine, they engaged in exchanging ribald stories.

Jupiter challenged his wife that she, and indeed all goddesses, demigoddesses, nymphs, and mortal women got more pleasure from lovemaking than their male counterparts.

The argument between the king and queen, though playful, became quite heated. The continued consumption of wine as they debated seemed to magnify the volume of their voices so that all Olympus rocked with the thunder of both the words and the laughter of the royals.

"You females," Jupiter contended. "You are the ones who get all the pleasure out of sex. We males are only around to squirt our seed in you. If you did not tempt us into your games of love, there would be no procreation. Ergo, you are created to take more pleasure from sex than males."

"What a stupid argument," Juno scoffed. "We females take interest in a hundred thousand different things. You males only have one thing on your minds. The only true pleasure you know is fucking and sucking. You spring your constant erections, force yourselves between our legs, shoot your little spurts, withdraw, and then think of nothing but who you are going to shag next."

Jupiter erupted into a gigantic laugh.

"Why Juno! What a preposterous statement! We males do spring our constant erections, as you say. We have all our pleasurable sensations centered in our pricks. You females are composed of so many pleasure areas that your pleasure in sex outweighs our own a thousandfold. You get pleasure from your breasts, from every inch of your skin, from your clitoris, your labia, your vaginas, your wombs... We have one orgasm in a session where you experience multiple orgasms..."

"Fie on your argument," Juno riposted. "Exactly the fact that your climaxes are centered in your peckers makes the experience much more intense than ours, defused as it is more generally in our bodies..."

And so the discussion went on and on. Respite was taken from the argument for a bit of sport on the royal couch. But as soon as the engagement climaxed, the debate was picked up again.

At length, the couple agreed that the debate could only be decided by a judge. The question was whether anyone could be an impartial judge in such a question.

The pair simultaneously came to the same conclusion. The judge would have to be Tiresias.

Tiresias was a double transsexual, and thus had experienced the pleasures of love from both sides. By a set of curious chances, at the age of twenty he was transformed by a pair of serpents who were mating in a green forest from a man to a woman. For seven years he experienced life in all its forms, including its sexual aspect, as a woman. At age twenty seven, wonderful to say, he happened to be hiking through the same forest and encountered the same two snakes, who were copulating in the same way. And behold! Tiresias was instantly transformed back into a man.

Who better to judge which of the sexes enjoyed the practice of love and romance more?

Mercury was sent down to Thebes where Tiresias happened to be. The god whisked the appointed arbiter to Olympus where he was informed of the task the two royal gods had set for him.

Tiresias listened to Jupiter's arguments. Then Juno expostulated on the other side. Tiresias allowed each side a rebuttal, pondered the arguments both from his personal erotic experiences as male and female, and delivered his verdict.

He declared that from what he had heard, and what he had personally experienced, he would have to rule in favor of Jupiter. Females, he ruled, had a far deeper physical, emotional, and exalted satisfaction from the act of love than their male consorts.

Jupiter was delighted and gloated.

Juno, however, was furious. She had never been a gracious loser. But in this case she was beside herself.

She condemned the judge to eternal blindness.

No god may ever undo the act of another. There would never be peace in Olympus were that not the case. But in return for his loss of sight, Jupiter gave Tiresias the power to know the future. And Tiresias became the most famous soothsayer in the world.

He lived to a legendary old age, consulted, respected, and rewarded by all the most powerful monarchs on earth.

CHAPTER VI

NARCISSUS AND ECHO

Jupiter had a short-lived affair with a glib nymph named Echo. The romance ended amicably enough, since Jupiter was not exactly the nymph's type. She preferred the pretty-boy type to a more majestic lover. She did, however, enjoy receiving trinkets.

Jupiter brought her up to Olympus and promised her unlimited trinkets if she would talk to Juno while he was carrying on his fuckfests down below on earth. Echo was always loaded with gossip and stories, and chatted incessantly. And Juno was so distracted by Echo that she missed keeping informed of her husband's philandering.

When Juno caught on to what Echo was doing, she expelled her from Olympus.

As a parting shot to the nymph, Juno said, "That wicked tongue of yours has tricked me many times. I am curtailing the power of your voice so that it can only repeat the last few words of whatever you hear others say."

Back in the glades of Boetia, Echo caught sight of the most beautiful youth she had ever beheld.

The youth was sixteen years of age. And he was much sought after by youths and maidens alike. But the young man, whose name was Narcissus, neither could nor would succumb to a fellow being. For he was much in love with himself.

He constantly caressed himself. He ran his fingers from the tips of his toes to the top of his head. His hands stopped to fondle his peter with great regularity. He moistened his nipples with his spittle and enjoyed the sensations that resulted from such massage. He inserted his fingers into every orifice that would receive them. He manipulated his hardon as frequently as Nature would give him release. No one on earth had ever before loved another as much as Narcissus loved Narcissus.

When the young man was traipsing through the fields, his hands caressing his body, Echo's infatuation for him reached epic proportions. She followed him by stealth and peeked at him from behind bushes, trees, and groves.

Finding himself alone on a lea, Narcissus shouted out, "Is anyone here?"

Echo called back, "Here!"

The lad looked around and called, "Come!"

Echo, of course, responded, "Come!"

Narcissus was intrigued. Who could be calling to him with such a sweet voice?

So he called out, "Let's meet!"

Echo was delighted. And she answered as Juno had allowed her, "Let's meet!"

Echo came rushing out from behind the copse in which she had been hiding.

She hastened towards her chosen lover with her arms outstretched to embrace him.

Narcissus was shocked at her approach. It was clear the nymph desired to throw her arms around him. That he could never allow. There was only one pair of arms worthy of such an action. That was his own.

He took off running to get away from the impetuous nymph.

She pursued, but when at last she had to admit to herself that she had been spurned, she gave up and sought someplace to hide and conceal her shame.

From then on, she has hidden in caves. Her love does not abate but causes her to constantly grieve.

Poor Echo wasted away until all that was left of her was her voice.

Narcissus happened upon a clear pool one day. The youth looked into the pool and saw a reflection of his magnificent body. He had been madly in love with himself before. But seeing his own beauty reflected up at him, he had the most tremendous erection of his young years. He was struck speechless as he saw the beautiful form in the pool engage in an act of self-love. He jacked off into the pool.

He knelt by the pool and gazed adoringly at the deep blue eyes. He was consumed with love. He attempted to kiss the rosy lips. He strove to embrace the swanlike, white neck.

He uttered promises of undying love to his reflection. He expressed his admiration for the noble nose, the splendid chest, the adorable dong. He bent down to kiss the cherry lips, only to get a noseful of water. He plunged his arms into the pool to embrace the handsome shoulders. He came up sopping.

When he smiled, his reflection smiled back. When he wept, tears flowed from the image in the pool.

He spoke to the golden image, "I love you."

Echo, speaking from her own heart, replied, "Love you."

Pining away for his lover he could not reach, he wailed, "Farewell."

The last sound he heard on earth was the response, "Farewell."

Narcissus perished in grief for his elusive lover.

When the nymphs and youths who had admired his beauty came to seek him, there was no body to be found. Where he had perished, there was only a flower. The flower with white petals surrounding their yellow center.

All that remained of the youth's beauty was the lovely narcissus.

CHAPTER VII

PYRAMUS, THISBE, AND THE HOLE IN THE WALL

Remarkably, among the tales of the gods transmuted into poetry by Ovid are some stories in which the Olympians have no role to play.

In his Book Five of *The Metamorphoses*, beginning at Line Fifty-five, Ovid relates the tale of the Babylonian lovers Pyramus and Thisbe.

Pyramus was the handsomest youth and Thisbe the most beautiful maid in the Orient. The gardens of their brick houses were separated by a tall brick wall.

As children, they played in the neighborhood roads and the hanging gardens. And thus, they could not remember when they had not been acquainted.

However, Pyramus' family and Thisbe's, although next-door neighbors, were not friendly. The feud between the two families was of ancient origin. So ancient that no one knew why the families hated each other any more.

Despite the feud, the children were good friends. They had to pretend to their parents that they did not meet or play together in the neighborhood. So the parents were none the wiser.

But as the children matured, their friendship bloomed into love. A love affair that had to be kept secret from their respective families.

In the wall that separated the backyard gardens of the two dwellings, there was a chink that neither family had noticed over the years.

But the eyes of love are ever resourceful. And the hole, which was somewhat lower than waist high, was the portal through which the lovers could speak, coo, and kiss if they knelt on the grassy turf next to the wall.

The lovers soon found that the hole in the wall was conveniently placed to allow them to fuck through it. And when they were quite certain their parents were engaged in activities that would prevent them from witnessing the acts of love that transpired at the back wall, the act was satisfactorily performed.

One day when the parents of the couple were away from home, the lovers met at the wall, kissed through the chink, and progressed on to their screwing.

Thisbe's father returned home unexpectedly to retrieve a tablet that was needed at his employment. He glanced into the garden and saw his daughter braced face-forward into the wall. He hastened into the garden to inquire what she was about.

"Oh, Father," Thisbe rapidly improvised. "The neighbors recently purchased a cow and are allowing it to graze in their garden. I have discovered that if I hold my twat up against this hole in the wall, the cow will run her tongue around it. Cow saliva happens to be the medication the physician recommends for female afflictions."

The father of course knew nothing about cures for female problems, so he bought the explanation without question.

"I did not realize we had a chink in the garden wall, Daughter. How long has it been there?"

"I wouldn't know, Father," Thisbe answered sweetly. "I just recently discovered it, and peeking through, I happily saw the cow grazing on the other side."

"Go back into the house, Thisbe," said the father. "I have been having rectal problems recently. I will see if the treatment that works for female ailments might be efficacious for my own distress." Thisbe quickly withdrew into the house.

She waited for her father's return.

Not much later, her father returned flustered.

"Daughter," he exclaimed. "I am going to have that hole plugged immediately."

"Why, Father?" she answered, alarmed that the source of her pleasure was soon to be obliterated.

"Apparently the neighbors purchased a bull, my dear. And not a cow. I held my ass up to the hole and the bull ran one of his horns into my asshole. I'm stopping up that gods damned hole tonight."

When her father had returned to his place of employment with his tablet, the sweethearts were conversing again at the opening.

When Pyramus understood that the hole would be stopped up, he proposed that they elope the following morning.

Thisbe agreed wholeheartedly.

They knew they would have to escape their homes at different times, depending on when their parents were sound asleep.

Rather than choosing a meeting place in the city where they might be apprehended, Pyramus suggested they get together in the shade of a mulberry tree near Ninus' tomb. The tree which they were each acquainted with was tall, with snow-white berries, close to a cool spring. Thisbe agreed that would be a fine place to meet.

That night, after her parents had retired, Thisbe crept to her parents' bedroom door and listened until she was quite sure the sounds within were the tonalities of sleep.

She stole out the door into the darkness without, made her way through the city and out into the countryside.

She found her way to the tomb without difficulty, and with her face still veiled to maintain anonymity, she sat under the mulberry tree.

In the distance, Thisbe observed a lioness crossing the desert, making for the spring. The beast's jaws dripped with the blood of a cow she had recently slain.

Thisbe fled to a near-by cavern and huddled within. But in her flight she lost her cloak, which lay on the desert floor.

After drinking at the spring, the lioness slinked back into the desert. But on her way, she came upon Thisbe's garment.

She muzzled the cape, leaving it stained with blood that still clung to her maw.

While Thisbe remained huddled in the cavern, awaiting the lioness' exit from the locale, Pyramus arrived at Ninus' tomb. He saw the tracks of the lioness and grew alarmed. When he came upon his beloved's blood-smeared wrap, he assumed the worst.

He was consumed with guilt, feeling that he should never have suggested such a dangerous place for their rendezvous.

He picked up the garment and carried it to a spot beneath the mulberry tree. He kissed the cape and cried copious tears into it. He drew his sword from its sheath and plunged it into his heart.

From the wound, the blood flowed from his veins into the earth and was drunk by the roots of the tree.

The tree's berries absorbed the gore and bear their purple hue to this day.

Thisbe emerged from her refuge, worried that Pyramus might have come and gone while she was hiding. Beneath the tree she spied a body writhing on the bloody ground. She approached and was appalled to see that the body was that of her lover.

She clasped her dying lover and mingled her tears with the blood oozing from his wound.

Pyramus, as his last living act, opened his eyes, looked upon the face of his beloved, and expired.

Thisbe observed her bloody cloak that was grasped in her Pyramus' hand and understood the fatal conclusion Pyramus had reached.

She spoke to the bloody form she held in her arms.

"You, my dearest, have died for love."

She took his sword in hand.

"Only death could part us," she continued. "But death shall re-unite us."

With these words she plunged Pyramus' sword into her own heart, and holding her lover in her tightest embrace, joined him in death.

When the bodies were found, the tale of their love-death was repeated throughout Babylon.

Tears flowed in the streets of all Babylonia.

And this sad, sad story would have been averted if only Pyramus had not cornholed Thisbe's father.

CHAPTER VIII

VENUS GETS PROPOSALS

Venus is the goddess of love, desire, and pleasure. But as popular as one would think this would make her, not every god was her friend. And she was touched by tragedy and difficulties as well as by bliss and rapture.

She was born from the foam of the sea, and was attended by Neptune's white steeds.

Jupiter swooped down and whisked her off to Olympus for she was clearly a new goddess thrust into the universe.

Venus stood among the assemblage of gods naked, beautiful beyond description, and dripping with the salt water from which she was born. The male gods were elated by the sight of the exquisite face, the yellow soft hair that extended below her knees, the ineffable breasts, the perfectly shaped belly, the magnificently formed ass, the legs shaped to perfection, and the beaver itself, the point of which pointed tantalizingly towards the golden garden of delights that constituted her cunt.

The virgin goddesses, Diana and Minerva, who eschewed the carnal love of males, preferring the dalliances of Lesbos, were as aroused as their male counterparts.

Venus, who was born with a deep vaginal itch that could be relieved only by a hard cock, threw back her head and laughed aloud at the attention she was receiving from the Olympian crowd.

She gave short shrift to the nude goddesses. Venus was born to swing one way, and one way only. And that way was towards the handsome, well-built, well hung naked male gods whose body parts were most notably raised in anticipatory greeting.

Juno took in what was transpiring in the throne room. Jupiter's regal dong was reacting and throbbing as heartily as that of every other masculine god. But he attempted to appear regal. Particularly since his wife was casting a baleful eye at him.

"Husband," Juno whispered. "You have to marry this one off fast. If she doesn't have a husband around to keep her in check, there will be Hades to pay here in Olympus. And down there on Earth as well, I dare say."

Jupiter immediately saw the wisdom of his wife's concern.

The voice of the king of the gods thundered out.

"Brothers, sisters, sons, daughters, and cousins. I see you are all impressed by the new member of our corporation. I want to welcome you, Venus, to our happy family."

Venus showered him with her most seductive smile. Jupiter noticed the frown on his wife's face. Juno was quite aware of the phallic response of her husband to the smile of the newest resident of Olympus.

Jupiter cleared his throat and continued.

"The lovely goddess will soon be wed. She will choose her own husband. So I call for all those who would be suitors to gather around her while all who do not wish to be considered draw back."

Jupiter and Juno ascended their thrones while the goddesses stepped away.

There was pushing, shoving, argument, and shouting among the suitors. The squabbling caused Venus to giggle and Jupiter to shout.

"Silence!" cried out the thunderous voice of the lord of the heavens and earth.

"You will press your suit and state your claim to the lovely goddess one at a time.

"Neptune, what would you have to say to lay claim to Venus as your bride?"

Neptune strode forth, trident in hand.

"I claim you, Venus, as my bride in the name of the sea. It was I who first welcomed you from the salty foam. Gifts aplenty I have for you. All the gems of the sea such as pearls and coral shall be yours. Grottos, seascapes, sunsets, typhoons, and dead sailors shall be yours. Accept my hand and become Queen of the Sea."

Venus snuggled up to the sea god and whispered in his ear.

"You turned me on, Neptune, from the moment of my birth." She gave a sideways wink towards his cock. "And it wasn't that trident of yours that caught my attention first." She punctuated the statement with another wink. "You have a terrific face, an impressive physique, and a majestic way about you. I am not going to marry you, but believe me, I'm going to show you a Hades of a time no matter who the sucker is who I choose for a husband. And I'm not talking about a one-night stand, either."

Neptune gave her a kiss on the cheek. Her promise of good times ahead sounded better to him than matrimony.

"Mercury," Jupiter bellowed. "Step forward and present your case."

Mercury bragged to Venus that his phallus was the envy of every god in Olympus. It was worshipped from India to far-flung Atlantis. He claimed to have the cleverest way with words, and knew all the gossip spilled at every crossroads of the world. What's more, he told her he had more tricks and jokes than any god or human, And, best of all, while the speediest of the gods, he was also the slowest in holding back ejaculations, thus prolonging the act of love for as long as his partner could stand.

Venus gave Mercury a whispered answer in his ear.

"Yes, Mercury. I spotted that gorgeous peter of yours as soon as I arrived here. I know as well that there are representations of it at every crossroads in the world. No god or man can rival it. But I would rather have that thing hung on a lover than on a husband. So, although I will not marry you, I promise you many a lively romp on the couch. And whoever my husband turns out to be, he'll never find out about our fuckfests."

The promise was more pleasing to the sliest of the gods than any prospect of matrimony. He exchanged winks with the beauty and retreated back into the crowd.

And so, one by one, the gods made their bid for the hand of the divine goddess. And she told each that while she would not be his bride, she would certainly be his lover.

Each, that is, except Apollo.

CHAPTER IX

APOLLO GETS REJECTED

Apollo was the last of Venus's suitors to make his case.

"Divine goddess," he began. "Your lyric beauty deserves as its mate only one as gorgeous as me. For I am not only the prettiest creature on earth, I am also the god of music and will celebrate your beauty in song forevermore. I am the god of the sun and you will be honored basking in my splendor. I deserve you because as husband and wife our combined beauty will stun the heavens and the earth."

Jupiter and Juno felt that the braggart had gone too far. Juno was particularly displeased since she never really cared much for Apollo. He was the fruit of one of Jupiter's earliest infidelities, the one with Latona.

Jupiter bristled at the suggestion that any god might outshine him.

Venus sensed the displeasure of the king and queen at Apollo's proposal. And was pleased. She did not particularly care for Apollo either and would certainly never consider being his bride.

She answered him softly, but loud enough to be heard by those who strained their hearing somewhat.

"I am sorry to have to tell you this, Fardarter. (This was a nickname employed by those who scoffed at the god who shot his darts far.) I don't have anything against guys who swing both ways. Everyone to his or her own sexual preferences. Even someone who does it with trees is all right with me – but not for me.

"But there's only one way I swing, and I don't get involved with gays or bis in a sexual way. So not only will I not marry you. Don't come knocking on my door next time you get a hardon."

Many of those who overheard Venus smiled snidely. Apollo himself was livid at being thus rebuffed and rejected by this newcomer, this parvenue, to Olympus. He retreated in as dignified a manner as he could. But in his heart, he vowed revenge.

Venus, although new to Olympus, was aware of the details concerning Apollo and Hyacinthus.

Quite recently Apollo had a tremendous crush on a youth named Hyacinthus. The youth was a splendid physical specimen. He was of a slender build, not overly muscular, and had a pecker that was of delicate rather then excessive dimensions.

Exactly the type of youth that set Apollo's heart a-flutter.

Apollo and Hyacinthus engaged in all manner of sport together. They went hunting together, bows drawn, hounds leading. They went fishing together, Apollo carrying the nets for the two of them. They hiked scented paths over mountain and across meadows, joining their voices in song. They practiced archery, played catch and quoits.

But the sport they most delighted in was the game of bunfuck. Hyacinthus had engaged in the sport with other youths with frequency. To do so with the radiantly beautiful god of the sun was his supreme delight.

Apollo's preferences in amatory games was catholic. He lent his heart and cock to nymphs, mortal females, goddesses, youths, satyrs, gods who were thus inclined, and, oh yes, trees.

The god and the youth gave themselves fully over to the game of love. Orifice met orifice. Protrusions also met orifices. Every orifice capable of welcoming any protrusion was entered. Any bodily part capable of being fondled was fondled.

There may have not been any more physical love affair on earth at the time than that in which Apollo and Hyacinthus engaged.

One day, the happy couple was practicing a game of quoits. Apollo heaved the discus with the strength and skill his godhood permitted. He loved to show off his skill for Hyacinthus, who was rightfully impressed by it.

The discus flew high into the air. Hyacinthus, with great excitement, ran forward to grab it, eager to return the throw. But, alas! The quoit struck the earth, rebounded, and hit the youth in the forehead.

He fainted. He fell.

Apollo rushed to his lover and tried to revive him. But he could not stanch the wound and wept as the lad died in his arms.

Hyacinthus' blood stained the ground, and from that spot a flower bloomed. The flower was deep purple in color. Apollo inscribed on the petals the word of his grief, "Ai, ai."

He named the flower Hyacinth.

There are those who believe the flower that Apollo wept over was the pansy, since that flower more resembles the one described by Ovid in his version of the tale.

But *Apollo and Pansy* hardly seems an appropriate title for the tale.

Although Venus rejected Apollo's suit because of his pleasure in both male and female lovemaking, she was too aware of Jupiter's infatuation with his cup bearer, Ganymede, to not make too public a statement about the reason for her refusal of Apollo's proposal.

CHAPTER X

VENUS DOES OLYMPUS

Juno was growing very restless. She felt that it was imperative that this new goddess get married. Not some time in the future, but right away. The newly arrived goddess had rejected the proposals of all the eligible gods...

But, wait a minute. There was still one god who hadn't made his bid. Her son Vulcan hadn't come forward. He was Juno's legitimate son, fathered by Jupiter in full legal wedlock. He was the god of fire and of artisans and smiths.

Perhaps, strangely, Venus might favor him as a husband. True, he was the ugliest of the gods, but he was the god who had bulging muscles and hair on his chest. True, he was lame, but he was always the most respectful of his mother of all the gods. Venus might just think that a good dutiful son might make a good, dutiful husband. And true, he was a bit stupid. But since he never had much to say, what difference did that make?

During the contest of the gods to marry Venus, Juno spied Vulcan cowering in a corner behind everyone else. He was ashamed to be seen. Not only because of his ugliness. But of all the gods, he was the least generously endowed with respect to his genitals. He had an awesome torso with the weewee of an infant.

Juno reached out from her throne with her long slender arm and dragged Vulcan forward to stand naked before Venus.

Before he could say a word, Venus looked him over. Gazing at his tiny thing, she smiled. The gods who were generously hung would be great lovers who could relieve her constant itch. For a husband, what she wanted was not size but docility.

Juno fairly shrieked at her son.

"Speak up, Stupid," she cried. "Tell the divine goddess why she should choose you for a husband."

Vulcan could not look Venus in the eye. Staring at her feet and blushing, he stuttered, "If you would like a husband who works late and far away, you should choose me."

"Come here to me, you gorgeous hunk of stuff," Venus invited.

The god of fire limped awkwardly up to the most beautiful goddess in Olympus.

Venus pulled his face down to hers and kissed him on the mouth with deep, ecstatic tongue penetration.

There, in front of the whole Olympian assembly, Vulcan sprang the most extensive boner he was capable of.

All the assembled gods broke out in applause. All, that is, except Apollo.

That very evening Venus and Vulcan were married.

And as the gods came forth to present their wedding gifts to her, Venus whispered to each of the males (except Apollo, of course) to tell him when she would be available for a round of sport on the couch.

The wedding night was quite exciting for Vulcan. The whole romp with her newly married husband was a total bore to Venus. But she suppressed her yawns and managed to show Vulcan the time of his life.

The next morning Vulcan hustled back to work. He had workshops underground at five volcanic islands – Lemnos, Lipara, Hiera, Imbros, and Sicily. He had urgent work at each, which kept him away from Olympus and his wife most of the time. Leaving Venus available for her favorite sport.

She scheduled her first engagement with Mars, the god of war.

Venus knew quite well what kind of lover Mars would be. Even if his reputation as a fierce, self-centered, brutal god was not common knowledge, one look at his arrogant swagger told her all she needed to know. But Venus was not adverse to the rough-stuff on the couch. Every form of lovemaking from the most nuanced to the most rugged gave her satisfaction.

He was the son of Jupiter and Juno and inherited the most violent qualities of each. His violent, savage character made him the most disliked god by the other Olympians, including his parents. None of that bothered Venus in the least.

Mars arrived late for his date with the goddess. He did not apologize for his tardiness. Rather, he blamed her for not having wine set out for him to get drunk on.

She told him, "The wine is over there on the table. Go pour your own wine."

Her interest was to provoke him, of course. And she was successful. He slapped her around some while he growled at her, "Don't you ever talk to me like that again, Bitch!"

Physically abusing his girlfriends was Mars' only form of foreplay.

Venus knew that many, many females were turned on by masculine brutality. She herself responded erotically, but sought out this form of amatory play only rarely.

Mars had her sit at his feet engaging sucking him off as he swigged down enough wine to make him roaring drunk.

"Get up here on the couch, Slut," he ordered. "I came here to fuck, not sit around on my ass and entertain you."

When she assumed the position, Mars assaulted her with fierce, ruthless thrusts. She found the approach stimulating enough to cause orgasm.

Mars slapped her face.

"Don't you dare come before me. I am Mars. And *I* come first.

Get it, Whore?"

Mars proved to be an indefatigable lover, whose persistence relieved Venus' deep itch again and again. So much so that she climaxed often, receiving a blistering slap each time.

All in all, it was a memorable bout. Not so much from the violence of the act as from the fact that Mars' ejaculations impregnated the goddess. In due course, she bore him a son whom she named Cupid.

But more about him anon.

Venus' next swain was Mercury.

Mercury was the son of Jupiter and Maia. He was by far the craftiest and subtlest of the gods. And possibly the cleverest.

He was the herald and the messenger of the gods. He was also the god of eloquence and fast-talking, of cunning and deceit, the god of roads and particularly of crossroads, of gamblers and thieves, and of liars. Venus thought him very cute.

Ten minutes before the appointed hour for their tryst, Venus heard the strumming of a lyre outside her chambers. She knew that Mercury had invented both the lyre and the love-song, and so had no question at all who was serenading her. Mercury's vibrant baritone voice was singing her praises. He lyrically described and praised her hair, her face, her eyes, her lips, her breasts, her arms... The song played on the goddess' vanity, which was immense. She loved the song and waxed romantic and sentimental throughout the recitation.

At precisely the moment agreed upon for their date, there was a soft knock on the door.

Venus opened the door and saw Mercury standing there. He was jauntily wearing his broad-brimmed, winged hat (the petasus), and his winged sandals. Those were his only articles of attire. He certainly would not wear anything that might hide his chief ornamentation, the one that dangled from his crotch area.

His vanity for his cock was as formidable as Venus' was for her entire body. Statues of his splendid peter adorned most of the crossroads of the ancient world.

In one hand he held a gorgeous bouquet of flowers and in the other his heraldic staff, the caduceus.

As he entered he complimented the arrangement of the boudoir and gushed at his paramour's beauty. The sweet-talk that ensued was eaten up by the vain goddess.

Mercury's seduction was as elegant as Mars' was crude. He maneuvered the goddess towards and onto the couch by a series of quips, light touches, gentle kisses, and unobtrusive hugs.

He did not thrust himself upon her but was continuous in exciting the one hundred twenty-three highly erogenous spots of the female body. Not once did he appear to have any concern for his own sexual needs or desires. He was totally intent on Venus' pleasure alone.

Not that his own state was hidden to the eye. And, as if by accident, when his hardon glanced over his lover's nude body, he attempted to appear demure. Nor, when Venus' hand lightly grazed his cock and balls did he object as he shuddered with delight and anticipation.

Venus was not caught by surprise when, by subtle application of tongue, finger, and even toe, he had laved her lips, armpits, neck, ass, asshole and cunt, he had raised her entire body to sub-orgasmic ecstasy, he slyly made his entry into her body. Not by the front entrance, but right up the ass. Such a sly fellow. Such a joker. Such an entertaining lover.

He excused himself, performed ablutions to the member that had glided up the tract of Sodom, and then proceeded to find one orifice after another to entertain with his love-wand.

During the course of the tryst, Mercury managed to fill the divine womb with bountiful amounts of his seed, none of the cells of which managed to come to fruition. His half-brother Mars had gotten there first and the result was already flowering into Cupid.

Out of delicacy, Ovid gives no fuller description of the fuckfest between Mercury and Venus. The translator would refer the reader to the poet's equally famous poems, the *Ars Amatoria* and his love poems entitled *Amores* for more lurid descriptions of lovemaking technique.

Venus' matinee was a double header. For Mercury had hardly made his departure when Neptune came calling at the boudoir door.

Neptune was the brother of Jupiter, and Juno, and Hades. (Yes, fair reader. Juno was not only Jupiter's wife, but his sister as well. Live with it.)

When the Olympian gods overthrew the old gods, the Titans,

Jupiter became god of the heavens and the upper regions, Hades became the god of the underworld, and Neptune the god of the seas.

Thus, of the gods that passed through Venus' portals on the first round, Neptune was the oldest and most sedate. He was also the only one who was married. He had to sneak away from his wife Amphitrite to have his rendezvous with the goddess of love. And he was the only one who never enjoyed a return engagement.

The sexual engagement of the god of the sea and the goddess of love fell somewhere between the love match orchestrated by Mercury and the rape-like style of Mars.

Neptune had been present at the birth of Venus from the foam. He had urged his son Triton to announce her birth with a blast of his conch horn. He had escorted her to Olympus. And he appeared to the goddess as being more avuncular than stud-like.

Neptune led her from her boudoir to his palace under the sea near Aegae in Euboea. Venus was as comfortable beneath the sea as in the air. And she enjoyed Neptune's erotic exchanges in the delightful buoyancy of the salt water. The fucking was staid and majestic, though with more passivity than excitement. Thinking to put some novelty into the action, he performed his trick of turning himself into a horse. However, Venus informed him politely that among the erotic practices she disdained, bestiality was near the top of the list.

So Neptune immediately regained his usual humanoid form, brought her and himself quietly to a gentle climax, thanked her politely, and returned her, dripping wet, to her boudoir on Olympus.

Venus did the gods who pleased her and kept Olympus a happy place indeed. At least as far as most of the male gods were concerned.

In the meantime, her husband, Vulcan, kept himself hard at work in his volcanic workshops.

However, when Venus bore Cupid, Vulcan came to Olympus to enjoy the role of the pleased father.

While he was there, doting on the darling little boy, the Cabiri, whose function was to spread doubt and suspicion, whispered in his ears and convinced him that Cupid had been sired not by himself but by his nephew Mars.

The great god of fire had been cuckolded. And he was enraged.

But the Cabiri advised him not to rage but to revenge himself on his wife and her lover. Yes, he was not shocked that his wife had enjoyed other lovers while he was at work. But to humiliate him by having a son that was not his... That was an affront that warranted revenge.

So the Cabiri, who are all-seeing and always ready to inspire mischief, told Vulcan to go to Apollo for help in righting the wrong to his dignity.

And when two gods like Vulcan and Apollo each have a hardon for someone, there's sure to be Hades to pay.

CHAPTER XI

THE REVENGE OF VULCAN AND APOLLO

When Vulcan came to visit Apollo at his palace on Mount Parnassus he was well aware that his half brother, who was chiefly the god of the sun, was equally known as the god who punishes. Thus, Apollo was always encountered bearing his bow and arrows.

When Vulcan told him his suspicions about Mars and Venus, Apollo was delighted. He would punish Venus for having rejected him when he proposed to her before the entire Olympian assembly. And he would be taking the high road in punishing Venus for... Well, whatever it was that was bothering Vulcan.

It happens that Apollo does see all things first. He sets out in his chariot, the sun, at dawn and gazes down on creation from on high until dusk. From his chariot he spied and scrutinized every spot where the two miscreants might be going at it. And sure enough, as he traversed the heavens above Thrace, he spied Venus and Mars wildly fucking up a storm on the banks of the Hebrus River. Apollo sneered down at the couple knowing that he would divulge their trysting spot to Venus' enraged husband.

When both Vulcan and Apollo had finished their day's work, they met secretly at Vulcan's smithy beneath the volcano of Imbros.

In the telling of what he had observed on the shores of the Hebrus, Apollo enhanced the scene. He painted verbal scenes of practices he knew would disgust Vulcan's sensibilities. He described coprophagy, golden showers, bestiality and sadomasochism. Not that Apollo found anything offensive in the practices himself. Having viewed every possible erotic act ever performed as he traveled across the heavens, he was immune to shock. As a matter of fact, he had practiced every form of sex, and found all of it to involve some degree of pleasure. But he knew his uncle to be somewhat squeamish, and so poured it on.

Vulcan's visage reddened to scarlet. His eyes bulged and his chin quivered with rage. He dropped his hammer, hitting his foot. The metal piece on which he had been working slipped from his grasp. Apollo could scarcely control showing the delight at the scene he was evoking.

Despite the rage and the pain, Vulcan set to work immediately to fashion a snare. He linked together bronze filaments and wove them into a net. The work was so fine no god or mortal could detect the net. The strands of a spider's web would appear gigantic in comparison.

The snare was fashioned to yield to the subtlest touch or movement.

Stealthily, Apollo and Vulcan sneaked to Thrace and spread the invisible net out on the spot the lovers had chosen for their frolics. There was no doubt the couple would return there at nightfall.

Predictably, the goddess and her paramour descended to Thrace as the moon rose. Venus dutifully spread her legs for Mars' assault as soon as her back hit the net that covered the ground. Mars, in full priapic propulsion, made violent entry into the awaiting sheath.

Instantly the net sprang around them, securing them soundly in the position of the two-backed beast.

Vulcan, meanwhile, limped to Olympus' heights with his son Triton in tow. He had Triton blow a voluminous blast on his horn, which roused all the Olympians to the great hall. From there, Vulcan led them to Thrace, to the banks of the river.

While the act of love is one of the loveliest sensations known, to an observer from outside it appears ridiculous and risible.

When Vulcan led the divine horde to view the coupling of his wife and nephew as they were entrapped in his web, the gods howled with laughter at the ludicrous sight.

However, the poet informs us that the joke fizzled somewhat. Both Mars and Venus were shameless. Venus did not see why being caught in an act of love could be amusing or shameful for the goddess of love. And Mars, having no sense of humor, did not understand or care about the laughter. The net had held him fast to his slut. So what? It added spice to the escapade.

Mars never thought about the situation again.

Venus was aware that Apollo was behind the prank and that it was supposed to be an act of revenge on his part. As far as she was concerned, the attempt was beneath contempt and not worthy of retaliation.

Venus solved her marital problem by having Cupid shoot a desire-arrow into Vulcan's heart so that he was forever so madly in love with his wife that he would excuse her infidelities so long as she submitted to his own carnal needs.

And, mortals have been assured by those who know that Venus never left her ugly, lame husband less than totally satisfied with his sex life.

CHAPTER XII

VENUS AND ADONIS

Venus' promiscuity with the gods of Olympus at times overshadowed the deeper nature of the goddess. For, although she was undeniably the goddess of heterosexual lovemaking, she was also, seriously, the goddess of love. And as such, she knew the meaning of true love.

The poets sang of Venus' abiding love. And strangely, it was not for a god, or even for a demigod. It was for a mortal.

One day, when Venus was sitting by the great Olympian pool, Diana came bustling by. Diana was Apollo's twin sister, and was the goddess of the moon. She was also the goddess of chastity and thus had interests at variance with Venus'.

Despite their differences, the two goddesses were friendly enough and enjoyed exploring the differences in their views.

During their brief discussion by the pool, Diana said she was on her way down to Arcadia to do some hunting.

Diana's chief interest was hunting. And accompanied by her nymphs was often seen in Arcadia in pursuit of game.

The goddess was fond of children, and was, in fact, a protectoress of boys and girls.

"Why don't you come down to Arcadia with me?" she asked Venus. "Bring Cupid with you. He loves to play with my hunting dogs and my nymphs and I always love to have him along."

If there was any pursuit or activity that left Venus cold it was hunting. She could see no point, pleasure, or purpose in chasing wild animals with bow and arrow. But she thought a trip to Arcadia would be fun. And Cupid did, indeed, enjoy playing with the dogs. And the nymphs who accompanied Diana always made a big fuss over him. And he basked in their attention.

So Venus and Cupid got into Venus's swan-drawn chariot and flew down to Arcadia accompanying by the hunting party.

The nymphs played with Cupid, Cupid played with the dogs, and Venus and Diana looked on with delight.

At length, Diana gathered her bow and arrows, and in her golden chariot set off in search of wild game. Her dogs and nymphs accompanied her up a mountainside in joyous chase.

The mother and son remained behind, playing riddles and cat's cradle, blindman's buff and hide and seek, patty cake and myriad other jolly games.

During the course of one of the games, one of Cupid's arrows fell out of its quiver and wounded Venus' bosom.

At first, Venus wasn't alarmed. She believed the arrow had only grazed her. But such was not the case. The arrow had actually caused a wound that penetrated well within her skin.

Towards midday Venus heard the baying of hounds and the sounds of the hunting party returning from the chase. And, spying the troop galloping down from the mountain she could see that a hunter and his dogs had joined up with Diana.

Venus' heart picked up an unusual beat. The love-arrow had performed its function. And Venus saw the youth riding down from the mount with the eyes of true love.

Diana and her entourage were ready to return to Olympus with their trophies of the hunt. Adonis, for such was the youth's name, desired to tarry by the stream and bathe away the grime of the chase.

Venus sent Cupid back up to Olympus with Diana and her crowd. All she desired to do was remain in Arcadia and gaze at her newfound love.

Adonis was not a modest lad, and entered the river while the beautiful goddess gazed on him with rapturous eye.

When he exited the river naked, Venus approached him and offered to dry him off with a towel which she caused to materialize on the spot.

Despite being a young male of astounding physical beauty, Adonis had experienced very little carnal knowledge. Venus' deftness with the towel soon had him in a heightened physical condition.

And there, in Arcadia, on the banks of the idyllic stream, Venus gave her swain his first delicious lessons in the art of love.

After a session of lively sport, while the couple panted on the grassy shore, Venus queried her lover about his interests.

And, as fate would have it, she learned that the lad had one obsession, and one only. The hunt.

In exchange for learning the art of hunting, Venus continued Adonis' education in the art she knew full well.

Venus could not resist the lure of the handsome young body. She caused him to lie down, spread-eagle, on a bed of flowers in a sylvan bower. She wafted her delicate fingers over his bronzed skin with the most delicate feathery touch. She knew which zones on his body were the most sensuous, arousing him to a state of ecstasy.

As his bulb emerged from the foreskin sheath, her velvet tongue traced patterns over its surface.

At the most propitious moment she enveloped the organ with her mouth and fairly sucked the jism out with a wild rush that came close to making the youth faint.

She then taught him the pleasure of muff diving. Adonis found the exalted pleasure of tracing paths up and down the goddess' twat, gradually approaching the pink bloom of her engorged clitoris. Then, applying much the same technique on that organ that his lover had lavished on his peckerhead, he brought her to orgasms that filled the bower with sighs, cries, and laughter.

Venus had mastery of all the arts of love which are enumerated by the poet Ovid. But her knowledge exceeded that of the poet a thousand fold.

Venus could not bear to leave Adonis' side. She did not return to Olympus, since Adonis, a mortal, could not accompany her there.

Before encountering Adonis, Venus' idea of a day in the country seldom went beyond lounging in the shade and cultivating her charms. Now her time was spent accompanying Adonis, following her dogs up hill and down dale in pursuit of stags, hares, and other safe game. Each hunt ended with joint baths with her youthful lover in streams, brooks, ponds or springs.

Venus was not without concerns, though. Adonis was a courageous hunter. He was not content to pursue the tamer prey. She was able to keep him from pursuing bears, boars and wolves. But only by promising him the most profound pleasures of love after the hunt if he hunted safely.

That was certainly incentive enough for the handsome youth to follow his beautiful lover's injunction.

Venus was pleased that her lover was following her dictates and avoiding exposure to dangerous situations. So following a morning of hunting and lovemaking, she felt secure enough about Adonis' safety to go to her palace on Cypress where Cupid was being attended by a band of Nereids who served as playmates.

Venus entered her swan-drawn chariot, exchanged a deep farewell kiss with her mortal lover, and drove off to her beloved island and her wanton son.

Adonis's love for his goddess was deep and sincere. But he was a spirited lad who had a strong streak of bravado. It was all very well to hunt deer, rabbits, and other harmless beasts when riding with his beautiful companion who rewarded him with myriad pleasures for complying with her strictures. It was quite something else to feel the thrill of danger when his love was far away over the sea.

No spirited young man worth his salt is going to cower from the real sport of the hunt. As long as Venus was not around to check, Adonis had to test his courage as he always had before Venus became his paramour.

As soon as Venus was borne out of sight by her swans, Adonis gathered his weapons, called his hounds, and mounted his steed. He yearned for danger.

The youth did not have to wait long before his blood quickened at the baying of the dogs. They had roused a giant, dangerous wild boar from his lair.

Adonis dismounted, raised his spear, took aim, and hurled. The weapon wounded the animal, but the fierce beast withdrew it with his slathering jaws and rushed at Adonis.

Adonis was separated from his horse and had to run. Alas! he was unable to outrun the enraged beast.

The boar's tusks gored into the lad's side, mauled him, and left him expiring on the ground.

Venus was still aloft when she heard the dying groans of her beloved. She immediately reversed course and landed back in Arcadia only to encounter the mortal remains of her true love.

From the young hunter's blood on the ground there sprang up a flower, which Venus named Anemone, which is to say Wind Flower

The goddess' grief at the loss of her lover sent her to the Gates of Hades. The gods of Olympus seldom visited the god of the underworld. Of the three great gods, Hades, who was also referred to as Pluto, was the least pleasant. He resented that his brothers Jupiter and Neptune ended up with more prestigious kingdoms than he. But since Venus was not directly related to either of his two brothers, he allowed her access to him.

Pluto, the kinder aspect of the god of the netherworld, in response to Venus' pleas, allowed Adonis to spend six months of every year upon the earth with her. And to this day, the goddess rejoices at his return at the vernal equinox.

CHAPTER XIII

SALMACIS AND HERMAPHRODITUS

The fruit of one of Venus' romances with Mercury was a son who was named Hippias by his mother. In the course of time, he assumed the name of Hermaphroditus. He is generally known to the poets by the latter name for reasons that will become apparent as we pursue Ovid's telling of the tale in Book Four of *The Metamorphoses.*

The lad was extremely fair of feature. His face bore all the beauty of his mother's visage, modified by the handsome masculine cast of his father's. And he inherited Mercury's splendid physique.

He was not raised on Olympus since, even though sired by a god and born of a goddess, he was not divine. He was fostered by a naiad who lived in a cave and who had five naiad daughters.

The daughters, like most naiads, were much given to masturbation. Their practice consisted not only of autoeroticism but also of the mutual variety.

As the only male living in the cave, Hippias was a happy addition to the practice, and an adept learner.

He engaged himself in the solo practice. But he equally enjoyed stimulating each of his foster sisters as well. Sometimes he fondled a naiad while he entertained his own organ. Sometimes he was fondled by one of the sweet things as she employed the other hand to her self stimulation. Still, on other occasions he and his partner were simultaneously engaged ith jacking each other off. On happy celebratory occasions, there were threesomes. The mechanics of this diversion are not revealed to us by any of the Latin poets.

When he arrived at the age of fifteen Hermaphroditus bade farewell to his foster mother Ida and to his playmates of the cave. He delighted in wandering into new lands and exploring foreign rivers, streams, pools, and springs. His goal was always to find exotic sweet waters since naiads are the nymphs of fresh waters and there was always sport to be had when he encountered foreign masturbatory partners.

On one fine day, the lad arrived at the land of Caria and found a lovely spot near Halicarnassus.

He spotted an inviting fountain and, of course, was attracted to it.

The water of the pool was so crystal clear the boy could see to its depth. It was bordered by lush grass.

And seated on the side of the pool was a naiad, Salmacis by name.

Her constant delight was to dangle her lovely legs in the pool, languidly comb her hair, and observe herself reflected in the pool as she engaged in fluffing herself off.

As she brought herself to a climax, she squealed, looked up, saw Hippias' approach, and hungered to involve him in mutual fondling.

She calmed herself, ran her comb through her gorgeous locks, smiled, and addressed her visitor.

"Welcome to my pool, you gorgeous hunk of stuff. Whether you be god or mortal, you are my kind of guy. Why don't you bring yourself over here and dangle yourself in my pond?"

Hippias accepted the invitation with alacrity. As he settled next to the nymph, her lips met his and her right hand met his love organ.

He responded by inserting his tongue into her waiting mouth and an index finger into her moist tunnel of love.

Thus joined, they slipped from the grassy bank into the inviting waters and caressed each other into a state of quivering orgasm.

The naiad kissed her newfound companion with unabashed passion, fondled him to renewed erection, playfully tweaked his nipples, and clung to his godlike body.

The naiad in her frenzy of love raised her face to the heavens and besought the gods with her prayer.

"O gods of Olympus who sent this gift of love to my pool, grant that from this moment on I may never be separated from my golden lover."

Hippias was as caught up in the ecstasy of the moment as his lovely partner. He added his endorsement to Salmacis' prayer.

"Oh, yes. If you, my divine parents, are attending to us, I add my voice. Let this nymph and me be inseparable and enjoy such pleasure forevermore."

Whether it was the lad's father, or mother, or both who responded, no mortal knows. But the prayers of the couple were granted.

The bodies of the lovers merged into one. The two faces became one beautiful image. The torso had both male nipples and voluptuous female breasts. The genital area sported the attributes of both sexes. From out of the pool into which two figures had descended, a single form arose, the body of Hermaphroditus.

Hermaphroditus wandered the world with a never fading smile. He encountered single-sexed individuals with whom masturbatory games of exotic complexity were enacted. Yet Hermaphroditus was able to find onanistic pleasures by fondling both his male and female attributes simultaneously.

The ancient sculptors left countless statues of Hermaphroditus for ensuing generations to enjoy. One can always recognize (him?) (her?) by the radiant smile on the lips.

CHAPTER XIV

PLUTO PLEASURES PROSERPINE

Ceres was the goddess of agriculture and of all plant life. She was one of the senior gods, the sister of Neptune, Pluto, Juno, and Jupiter. There was, as we know, no restriction against relations between brother, sister, niece, nephew, etc. Among the gods there was ample sexual frolicking on Olympus, and indeed, anywhere at all.

On one merry occasion Jupiter impregnated his sister Ceres. And Ceres conceived and bore a lovely daughter she named Proserpine.

Pluto ascended from his dark domain and was in Olympus when his niece was born. He was dazzled by the beauty of the child and told Jupiter he wanted her to be his bride when she attained maturity.

Jupiter, without thinking to ask Ceres what she thought of the proposal, agreed that Proserpine would be Pluto's bride at an appropriate future date.

Jupiter never got around to informing Ceres about the transaction.

Years passed and Proserpine matured into a lovely maiden. Which, as so often happened, annoyed Venus. The goddess' vanity stirred envy within her if she thought any other creature's beauty rivaled hers.

(Yes, Proserpine's beauty really was that awesome.)

In the vale of Enna, on the island of Sicily, Proserpine was gathering posies.

At the same time Pluto became concerned. There was a violent shaking that rumbled through his kingdom of Hades. The quake was caused by the Titans who are held captive in Tartarus. Tartarus is as far below Hades as the heavens are above the earth. Pluto could not determine whether the rumble came from above or below, but was most worried that his kingdom might be invaded by the light of day and determined to ascend to earth to check out the situation.

He mounted his black chariot, whipped the black horses that led it, and burst up to earth.

As Pluto emerged onto the earth's surface, Venus observed the lord of darkness. She had just cast a jealous eye on Proserpine, and a plot sprang into her mind.

She smiled her wickedest smile. She had never much cared for Ceres, thinking her far too goody-goody for her own good. And her hatred for Proserpine always seethed within her.

She called Cupid to her side. Cupid fluttered near her, sensing a chance to engage in some delicious mischievous act.

"Son," she said. "Look down there on earth. Do you see the vale of Enna?"

"Of course, mother," he replied. "They say I am blind. But, as you may be aware, that is merely a metaphor. You see..."

Venus was not interested in hearing the little twerp discourse on metaphors and cut him off.

"Yes, yes, I know all about that," she snapped. "You will notice that Pluto has come out of his dismal realm and is approaching the vale. And, note, what's more, that that dreadful creature, Proserpine, is prancing about in that very area. Take your bow and arrows down there and do something nice and wicked for Mommy."

Cupid, ever wanton, ever sportive, was off in a flash.

When Pluto arrived face to face with Proserpine, he was not aware immediately that this was the bride Jupiter had promised him. Not that it would have made any difference because Cupid unleashed on him an arrow dipped in essence of buggery. Rear entry was always Pluto's choice of diversion anyway. But the arrow carried the nectar of true love with it as well.

Cupid then, nearly simultaneously, aimed an identical arrow at Proserpine. She fell in love with the darkly handsome god and yearned for anal penetration from his enormous, engorged dick.

There, on the flower-strewn grasses of the vale, Pluto made his entrance up the ass to the delighted shrieks of his promised bride.

All concerns about the rumbles that had sent Pluto on his investigative tour of earth vanished. The couple coupled in their preferred manner until sunset with Venus and Cupid looking on in absolute delight.

Pluto urged his bride to enter the chariot, which she did most willingly. She first picked up the bouquet she had been gathering to take with her to the kingdom below where she would be queen.

When the couple arrived at the shore of the Cyane River, the chariot stalled. The god struck the river bank with his trident. The earth made an opening on the spot, giving Pluto and his bride entry to the underworld.

True joy does not exist for the shades who dwell in Hades. However, when Pluto is cheerfully cornholing Proserpine, the dismal realm becomes somewhat less glum. Not that hope is expressed by Hades' inhabitants. All hope is shed before entering that realm. But some lifting of oppression and depression is sensed on the occasion of the king cornholing his queen. And, happy to relate, the royal union is frequent.

Ceres was devastated that her daughter seemed to have disappeared entirely. She searched the world over, and found not a trace or a clue. She sought the advice of Apollo, Aurora, and Hesperus who observe everything on earth in the course of the day. But to no avail.

Still, undaunted, Ceres pursued the search for her daughter. She left no land untrod, and no sea or river uncrossed.

At length she returned to Sicily and stood by the banks of the

Cyane where Pluto had gained re-entry to the dark domain.

Ceres observed the fissure in the earth and instantly knew where her daughter was.

She concluded that the earth itself had swallowed her daughter and thereupon she cursed the soil.

Ceres had endowed the earth with fertility, and now, in return, the earth had seemingly betrayed her.

As a consequence of the goddess' curse the seed failed to germinate, nothing would grow but thistles and brambles, animals died, drought prevailed, and it appeared that life would no longer grace the earth's surface.

The gods on Olympus were alarmed at the devastation down on earth, and Jupiter sent Mercury down to summon her.

Ceres explained to her brother Jupiter the cause of her bereavement.

Jupiter was anxious to intervene. He told his sister he would allow Mercury to go to Pluto's realm to demand Proserpine's release. But he informed her that the Fates had decreed that no being who had dwelt in the underworld could come back up to earth or beyond if he or she had partaken of any food while in the dark realm.

Mercury flew down to Pluto's netherworld and informed him of Jupiter's demand.

But Pluto had previously offered a pomegranate to his bride and she had sucked the sweet pulp from a few seeds.

So Pluto, with a rare smile, informed Mercury that he would willingly comply with his brother's request. He would not allow that he was subject to any demands from one he considered his equal, not his superior. So he claimed the release of the nymph was simply an act of generosity on his part.

Proserpine, who sat on the throne next to her husband informed the messenger that she had swallowed a bit of juice from the pomegranate.

The Fates were consulted. There was no countermanding their decision.

On weighing the case, the Fates determined that the miniscule amount of juice Proserpine had tasted merited a compromise. And that Proserpine could join her mother for six months out of every year. But she had to return to her husband for the following six months.

So, from the vernal equinox to the autumnal equinox, Proserpine dwells with her mother and the earth is fruitful. From the autumnal equinox to its counterpart in Spring, she returns to her husband's realm while the earth lies fallow.

Proserpine, however, to Venus' displeasure, is happy both when on earth with her mother and when in Hades with her husband.

Mother's love is all very well. But, her asshole misses Pluto's big cock sorely during the six months she must sojourn on earth.

CHAPTER XV

CUPID'S PSYCHE GETS SHAGGED

Three beautiful daughters were born to King Calpurnius and Queen Tiana. The youngest of the three, but by far the loveliest, was named Psyche, which, in the Greek tongue, signifies *butterfly.*

Such beauty was painfully offensive to Venus. Particularly because the mortals down on earth were deserting her altars and paying more attention to Psyche than to her. The vulgar crowd even began calling Psyche a Venus.

"This is just too much to bear," Venus complained. "I swear, that girl is going to repent of that beauty she's flaunting."

The goddess called her winged son, Cupid, to her side.

She pointed out Psyche to him and vented her spleen.

"Just look at that proud beauty," she sneered. "I want you to go down there and punish her. I enjoin you to wreak revenge on her for Mommy Dearest. You just shoot one of your wickedest arrows into her beautiful bosom. I want her to fall deeply in love with as ugly, as disgusting, as hideous a being as any that walks the earth. And I want this one to turn out better than that job you did on Proserpine. If you know what's good for you, that is. Now go make Mommy proud of you."

Cupid was always ready to play mean pranks on mortals. Especially if it would bring him nice rewards from his mother.

He filled his vials with the potions appropriate to the commissioned task and flew down to Psyche's boudoir.

When he arrived, the maiden was slumbering peacefully. She was stark naked and Cupid, despite himself, felt a pleasant tingling in his balls.

He decided he would not have to begin by using his arrows. He emptied a few drops of a bitter potion onto the sleeping lovely's lips. She absorbed the potion while remaining asleep.

Cupid tipped an arrow with the elixir of true love and touched Psyche's side with the tip. At the touch, the maiden, startled, suddenly awoke and stared directly at Cupid. He was, of course, invisible. But he was so jarred that he inadvertently wounded himself with the arrow he was holding.

Infused with love, the wanton winged boy flew back off to Olympus.

The first drops Cupid had spilled into her mouth guaranteed that no mortal other than a monster would seek her hand.

Psyche's sisters, who were far less lovely than her, found royal suitors for themselves and were happily married. Psyche, realizing that she had offended Venus, remained in solitude and yielded herself to her fate, though having come to lament her beauty.

But Psyche did have a lover who came to her chambers every evening. And she received this divine lover, nay, welcomed him willingly to the charms and pleasures of her exquisite body.

Cupid arrived only in the darkness of night. And he was gone before Aurora, the goddess of the dawn, announced the coming of daylight.

Cupid, who was deeply in love with Psyche, stole away from his mother's view and descended to Psyche's bedroom as soon as Hesperus announced the approach of night.

When Cupid arrived for his first visit, Psyche was not alarmed. Although she could not see the visitor, she was enthralled by his beautiful voice.

When he requested her to submit to be bound by the gossamer threads he wrapped about her wrists and ankles, she yielded without question.

For Psyche, though she had never seen his face, had fallen deeply in love with Cupid when she had looked toward his invisible face after the arrow head had grazed her. And in turn, Cupid had fallen as deeply in love with Psyche when she had awakened after he wounded himself with his arrow.

In the dense darkness, the maid trusted her phantom lover. He extended the gossamer threads he had slipped around his paramour's wrists and ankles to the four corners of her bed. She was held in total bondage. And yet she knew that if she were to resist and pull away, the bonds would break and she would be free. And she would lose her lover forever.

Cupid, his wings fluttering softly, hovered above her extended body. He lowered his lips to hers and gently, softly, kissed her. The welcome of her lips informed him that her body was his to caress as he pleased.

He flew over her face and caressed her hair with his warm breath. He nuzzled her entire nude body with his finely feathered wings. She shivered and tossed lightly, but always making sure not to break the bonds that so lightly held her.

Cupid traced paths over her entire exposed body with his hard prick and soft balls. She shivered with delight as she sucked his cock.

Continuing to hover above her, supported by his wings, he made love to her mouth with his genitals. She returned the lovemaking with gurgles of delight.

When he entered her love channel, the ecstasy nearly overcame them both. But not to the extent that Psyche broke the strands with which Cupid had bound her.

Night after night the godling returned to the earthling's boudoir. Each time Psyche yielded to the gossamer bands. On each return trip Cupid varied the lovemaking techniques made possible by his ability to fly, float, and hover.

Cupid sang to Psyche with accents of love. Psyche learned to join him so that divine melodies accompanied the sexual congress of the immortal with the mortal.

Psyche often begged her lover to remain until daybreak that she might behold him. But he would not, and, indeed, could not do so.

He informed her that under no circumstance must she endeavor to see him.

"Why would you need to behold me?" he asked. "Is not my love for you plain enough? Were you to see me, you might fear me, you might adore me, but all I ask is that you love and trust me. For I would rather that you know me as an equal to you in love, and not adore me as a god."

Psyche's sisters came to visit her one day, and she confessed to them her relationship with a divine or semi-divine lover.

The sisters, who had always been jealous of Psyche, strove to convince her that her lover insisted on remaining in the dark because he was a monster.

The sisters offered Psyche spiteful advice.

"Have a lamp available at your bedside," they urged. "Also keep a sharp knife under your pillow. Lull him to sleep, when, while he is dozing in post-coital contentment, you light your lamp and see whether he be god or monster. If he is the monster we believe him to be, behead him with the knife and save yourself from his depredations."

The wicked advice festered in Psyche's head, and, the suggestion became irresistible.

So she filled her lamp and sharpened her knife. The lamp she placed on her bedside table and the knife she hid under her pillow as her sisters had suggested.

That night, midway through their embraces, Psyche crooned her lover to sleep.

Whilst he slept she lit her lamp and beheld not a monster but the most beautiful of the gods.

As she leaned over to observe the body of her lover with close attention, a drop of the flaming oil spilled onto his shoulder. His eyes sprang open and beheld Psyche. He spoke not a word, spread his wings, and flew out the window.

Psyche was devastated. She recognized immediately that love cannot live alongside suspicion.

Psyche set out to find her lover and beg forgiveness for her suspicion. She wandered wherever her lovely feet would take her, ingesting hardly any food or drink.

Psyche determined at last that only Venus could assist her. Since it was Venus' son she had disappointed, perhaps Venus herself, who was, after all, the goddess of love, would intervene.

Venus, with vengeance still in her heart, set task after task for Psyche to perform. Psyche became more and more debilitated by the dangerous tasks, but persisted in carrying out the demands of the goddess.

Cupid looked down on Psyche's pain and discouragement and knew that he could not abandon his love. For the love had never abandoned his heart.

Cupid went directly to Jupiter and pleaded for clemency for Psyche.

Jupiter, who was nearly always sympathetic towards the act of love, pleaded Psyche's case with Venus, promising her the gift of the evening star if she would relent.

It may have been her soft heart, or, perhaps, cupidity for the brilliant star, that convinced Venus to relent.

But relent she did.

And the lovers were reunited on Olympus and wed for perpetuity.

And their union produced a daughter, whose name is Pleasure.

The story of Cupid and Psyche has been explained away by philosophers, sages, and even ecclesiastics as a great allegory about love and the human soul. For these wise men are keenly aware that the word psyche in Greek means both *butterfly* and *soul*.

But I have translated the story from the Latin, not Greek, and do not hold with that. So I present the tale simply as a love story.

Make of it whatever you will.

CHAPTER XVI

A POET'S FOOTNOTE

The Latin poets like Ovid who provided ensuing generations with tales of the ribald acts of the gods did not possess the modern blessing of the footnote.

If they had, the explanation of the relationship between Hebe and Ganymede would have survived as merely a couple of footnotes in the amatory poetry of the first century.

Within the body of the other poets' works we find that Hebe was a daughter of Jupiter and Juno. She was not a particularly blessed child and was given the job of waitress to the gods and goddesses. In particular she filled their flagons with nectar, the only liquid any self-respecting deity will consent to quaff other than the occasional cup or two of wine.

Juno tried to comfort her by telling her she was the goddess of youth. But the title did not do much for Hebe who thought she was the recipient of the short end of the stick.

She was anxious to get out of the job of cup-bearer, but feared she was stuck with it for eternity.

Luck fell her way on the day Jupiter's eye fell on Troy and he spied Ganymede there.

Now Jupiter, like his son Apollo, was omnisexual. He would fuck females, be they goddesses or mortals, beasts (both sexes), or, occasionally boys. (However, he was never caught doing it with a tree.)

Ganymede was as beautiful a boy as Psyche was a girl. To Jupiter, he was irresistible. The kid gave him a hardon.

So the king of the gods personally took on the form of an eagle and whisked the lad up to Olympus.

But what to do with the boy? He couldn't just hang around doing nothing.

Oh, Jupiter had definite plans for him at bedtime. But he had to give Ganymede a job during the daytime.

By chance, Jupiter had recently brought Hercules up to Olympus and conferred immortality on him. But Juno insisted that the big lug get married off to keep him from disrupting the peace of the palace.

Hebe was moping about and wasn't really much of an addition to the Olympian parties as she slouched about reluctantly filling the flagons. But her eyes lit up whenever she sidled up to the muscle-man who had recently become a tenant of the palace.

So Jupiter married his daughter Hebe off to Hercules and filled the spot of cup-bearer with Ganymede.

And henceforth Ganymede not only filled cups during the daytime, he comforted Jupiter's bed at night. For Jupiter could never get enough of buggering the lad.

And, from the viewpoints of the gods, there was general delight that the new cup-bearer was not grumpy like Hebe but full of smiles and good cheer.

And not bad to look at, either.

CHAPTER XVII

PASIPHAE GETS SHAGGED BY A BULL

Pasiphae was one of Apollo's daughters, and thus immortal. But she never even considered dwelling on Olympus. She considered Earth her home and never ventured up into the heavens or down into the netherworld.

She married Minos, the king of Crete and emperor of the Cretan empire and bore him three children, Androgeus, Ariadne, and Phaedra.

Pasiphae's sexual needs extended beyond Minos' embraces. But in addition to being a goddess, she was a magician and sorceress, so devised a potion she took before fucking when she wished to avoid conception.

Minos was minimally endowed in the phallic department. He just barely managed to worm the tip of his weewee into his wife's abundant hole. But, as mentioned, he did manage to sire three progeny.

For Pasiphae, like Europa, size did matter. Her cunt craved ripe dicks that were long and thick, from which bold balls hung.

She scoured her island kingdom, and indeed her Minoan empire, in avid search for husky, well-hung males.

But alas! No phallus ever quite filled the queen's need. And an unsatisfied queen is not a happy queen.

She left hundreds of young men feeling sexually relieved, yet sadly inadequate where it counts.

King Minos had a favorable relationship with Neptune. Indeed, it was Neptune himself who had secured Minos' uncontested right to the Cretan throne.

Minos expressed the desire to sacrifice a worthy bull to Neptune as a thanks offering. And Neptune obliged by sending the king a magnificent white bull.

Now Minos had a despicable side to his character. He was inordinately fond of the handsome bull and could not bring himself to kill it simply to please the god.

"Neptune isn't the brightest god around," he thought. "I have a very fine white bull out in the pasture. I'll sacrifice that one instead."

And so he did.

The bull from the sea was put to pasture on the finest meadow in Crete, where only the choicest heifers grazed contentedly.

Oh what a time the white bull had. And how the heifers rejoiced at the servicing he provided them with.

One day, when Pasiphae was scouting the island for a suitable partner, she happened upon the pasture.

Standing apart from the heifers, the bull from the sea portrayed a majesty that took Pasiphae's breath away. The bovine was pissing tumultuously. Even such a routine act seemed awesome to the goddess-queen. The size of the organ astounded. The pendulous testicles were close to inspiring. She felt herself damp below. In short, Pasiphae had fallen in love. Love at first sight.

She had to feel that enormous pizzle pleasure her insides. She grew increasingly damp.

She had to attract the bull's engorged attention. But how?

She maneuvered around so the bull's eyes were directed at her. She raised her robe, displaying her oozing cunt.

No response from the bull-from-the-sea.

She faced away, displaying her notable buttocks. She wiggled the bare globes at the bull. She shimmied the alluring backsides in a suggestive way that had caused many a male to explode in orgasm.

The bull was clearly bored with the display.

A heifer who appeared to Pasiphae to be rather ordinary in appearance displayed her obviously ready cunt to the stalwart bull.

Bull's eye!

In a trice the bull was erectile and mounting the cow.

What an awesome sight!

Pasiphae was left with a finger up her twat and her thumb massaging her clitoris.

This was not the finale she had envisioned when she first spied and fell in love with the white bull.

Severely dejected, she observed the bull discharging his powerful seed into the heifer. Pasiphae could swear the cow was smiling with a satisfied expression on her maw.

To be jealous of a cow! What an indignity!

Pasiphae was dejected. And yet, in a happy moment, she had an inspiration.

Daedalus was the greatest artisan of the age. He had even fashioned wings composed of wax and feathers. He had devised the motions that enabled him to fly by subtle motions of the wings. But the results from that invention are dealt with by Ovid elsewhere. And we are concerned at this point with translating what he has to say about Pasiphae's dilemma.

Since Daedalus was the most cunning craftsman of his age, and since he was employed by King Minos, and this, by extension, by Queen Pasiphae, he was clearly the person to be consulted about how to cause the bull to respond to the queen's love and lust.

Daedalus did not ask any embarrassing questions. He was up to the task.

He constructed a hollow wooden cow that would just fit around Pasiphae's shape. The back of the model was left open, so that Pasiphae's female ass and twat would be exposed to the open air and available to the lust of the animal.

He then covered the construction with a cow's pelt, so that the ensemble really did appear real.

Pasiphae fit into the contraption quite comfortably and had a couple of her slaves set it up in the meadow where the bull-from-the-sea grazed and frolicked.

The queen sent her slaves away, but there is a rumor that they hid in a copse to see what in the world their mistress was about. It may have been they who, as witnesses, told the story as it came to the ears of the poet generations later.

Pasiphae managed to manipulate herself around the meadow as though grazing. She got in position where her bare ass was directly in line with the white bull's vision. She wiggled that attractive part of her anatomy as suggestively as she knew how.

The bull's attention was certainly attracted. He had never seen a more attractive sight in his life.

For the first time, Pasiphae wondered whether the bull would find the right entrance. She did not worry about it, though. If he missed her cunt and went up her ass with that magnificent hard cock the first time, that would be a thrill in itself. She would simply return again and again until her bovine lover got it right.

Yikes! Oh yes! The bull mounted her royally and inserted that grand pizzle exactly where the queen wanted it. Wow! Ecstasy!

It must be told at this point that Pasiphae had not taken her contraception potion that morning. She was madly in love with the heroic bull. She desired to receive his seed without dilution.

And, indeed, her womb was filled fuller of his sperm than she had even imagined possible.

Pasiphae was blissfully happy. The bull enjoyed the ride, withdrew, and went on to graze contented in his pasture as his goddess-queen lover extricated herself from the contraption and skipped joyfully back to the palace.

The bull-from-the-sea and Pasiphae trysted in the meadow frequently. Well...daily. Well...even more often.

And the queen conceived.

In due course, Neptune decided that he wanted his bull back and the white bovine returned to the submarine stables.

During the gestation period Pasiphae mourned for her lover, but knew that towards the end of her pregnancy she would not have been able to entertain him anyway.

She bore a child with a human body and with the head, shoulders and genitals of a bull. She named him Minotaurus.

King Minos doubted that the issue was his. Pasiphae answered him indignantly.

"Of course Minotaurus is yours."

"But he doesn't resemble me at all," the king responded.

"That is your fault, not mine," Pasiphae told him. "Neptune sent you that white bull. You played a trick on him and sacrificed a second-rate one. Neptune was incensed and not only called back the bull but put a curse on you for your impiety. His revenge was to cause you to ejaculate this monster into my womb. Well, he's our little boy and we'll just have to love him all the same."

Minos had his doubts. But what could he do?

Pasiphae nursed Minotaurus for two years. And she, and her husband, and the entire court noticed that little Minotaurus became quite ferocious as he matured.

When Pasiphae weaned him from her breast she tried to find solid food to feed him. But her son informed her that all he would eat was human youngsters.

Pasiphae fed him cast-off younger lovers and Minos fed him prisoners from his wars.

Eventually Minos, an emperor after all, required his vassal states to send him children to feed Minotaurus.

It was not safe for Minotaurus to wander freely around the palace. He kept eating stray youngsters.

So Minos called on his chief craftsman, Daedalus, to solve the problem.

Just outside the palace gates Daedalus constructed a labyrinth to enclose the minotaur.

It was most cunningly and intricately made. Not only did the innumerable passages wind, twist, and repeat on themselves, they led to blind ends that were decorated with changing designs so the wanderer arriving at the same dead-end repeatedly was under the impression that he was in a spot he hadn't seen before. The eye was constantly deceived not only by the unusual conflicting passages but by the confusing murals.

The victims to be sacrificed to the minotaur were forced into the structure by a contingent of Minos' soldiers. Once in some hundred paces, they were shunted off into various passages. The captain in charge was able to lead his men back out by having been instructed by the architect. The victims, however, not knowing the secret of the hundred paces were doomed to wander in confusion until meeting with Minotaurus.

The bull-man enjoyed the pursuit of his prey. The hunt kept him amused. And as he tracked the victims down one by one, his hunger grew, making the feast on the sacrifice that much more satisfying.

Pasiphae had it up to here with Crete. She had shagged every male available and none satisfied her vaginal demands. So off she went, leaving her husband Minos to deal with Minotaurus.

She wandered (and may be wandering still) throughout the world for a phallus as satisfying as that of the bull-from- the-sea.

When the god Bacchus visited India, he met a fellow god there by the name of Ganesh. Ganesh had the head and shoulders of an elephant but the body, cock, and balls of a human.

It just makes one wonder.

CHAPTER XVIII

THESEUS: CAD, LOVER, PAL

Theseus was a great hero. And like so many heroes he was brash, rude, callous, crude, a bully, and a cad. He was very attractive to the fair sex. And he had a motto which he applied to every female who worshipped him. *Fuck 'em and forget 'em.*

And the gods loved him. He was so much like them.

Everywhere he went, the women went crazy for him. Such is a hero's life.

After a number of adventures in which he was able to kill, maim, or incapacitate tyrants, robbers, or others he deemed miscreants, he arrived in Athens looking for heroic acts to achieve.

The king of Athens at the time was Aegeus. Unbeknownst to either Aegeus or Theseus, they were father and son. You see, Theseus was a bastard in more ways than one.

There was a silly to-do about a sword Theseus was carrying that was the cause of the two men recognizing the paternity issue. Theseus' step mother, Medea, tried to poison him, and when she failed, took off for Asia.

That left Theseus with his father, bored and looking for some kind of adventure where he could show again how heroic he was.

Athens, at the time, was a vassal state in King Minos' empire. And, as such, was forced to pay tribute to Minos of seven youths and seven maidens to provide a tasty meal for Minotaurus, a monster dwelling in a Cretan labyrinth.

When the time came when the fourteen Athenians were to be shipped off to Crete to satisfy Minotaur's hunger, Theseus told his father he wanted to be sent as one of the seven youths.

King Aegeus protested, of course. But Theseus persisted.

"Father," he said. "There is only one way a stop can be put to this mad tribute you pay to that tyrant, King Minos. The minotaur must be slain. I have successfully triumphed over Vulcan's bastard son Perphetes and some score of petty tyrants and marauders. Even that arch evil-doer Procrustes I slew with my sword. I am acknowledged as a hero by all the known world. Would you deprive me of proving myself for the glory of your kingdom, Athens? If I remain behind while fourteen of your subjects are sacrificed to the Minoan monster I will be disgraced."

Aegeus yielded to the argument and allowed his son to be one of the Athenians sent as tribute.

En route to Crete, his thirteen Athenian companions hailed him as the most heroic prince Athens had ever had. For as Aegeus' son, Theseus declared himself prince.

None of the seven maidens arrived at the Cretan shore still virgins. The seven lads had only themselves to enjoy sexually along the way. Theseus took full advantage of the maidens, whether they all wished to fulfill his libidinous needs or not. There was one who resisted at first, but she was beaten into submission by the hero.

When the ship arrived at the island kingdom the fourteen sacrificial victims were hauled nude before the royal court at Cnossus.

When the eye of Minos' daughter, Ariadne, fell on the gorgeous physique of Theseus, she fell in love on the spot. Theseus had that effect on sensual females and was immediately aware that he could fuck the princess if he could get to her couch.

He even knew he could have her if only he and she could hide behind one of the many columns and pillars that supported the palace.

No such opportunity presented itself, for the youths and maidens were marched off to the dungeons where they were to be kept until the morrow when they would enter the labyrinth to entertain and feed the minotaur.

It was well known that Minotaurus preferred to deflower virgins before devouring them.

Ariadne convinced the dungeon guards that her father, the king, had sent her to inspect the imprisoned maidens to see if they were truly virgins as certified by King Aegeus. If not, the tribute from Athens on the following round would be doubled for each defective girl.

The princess thus gained easy access to the underground prison, passed by all the young ladies and found the handsome Theseus.

Theseus somehow felt that the princess would find him. The adoration he had observed in her eyes as she gazed in rapture at him in the palace assured him of it.

The thirteen other prisoners modestly averted their eyes while the prisoner-prince shagged the Cretan-princess. As usual, the copulation was short-lived, since Theseus simply quickly ravaged Ariadne. She did not need more. And he, as usual, made short work of fucking.

"How do I get out of this mess?" he asked the star-struck piece of ass.

"Will you be able to slay the minotaur once you find him in the labyrinth?" she asked.

"Of course. I am invincible," Theseus bragged. "All I have to be able to do once I've done him in is get out of the damned labyrinth and then find a boat to get me out of this gods damned island."

As it turned out, Ariadne had the solution to her lover's dilemma. She had brought with her a clew of thread. She told him that he needed to fasten one end of the spool to the entrance of the labyrinth, then follow it back to its source when he had finished his job.

Further, she told him she would be waiting at the entrance when he came back, lead him to a boat that was waiting in the harbor, and then they would sail off to be together for the rest of their lives.

Theseus sneered, unseen by the princess, and said, "You bet.

Baby."

Theseus latched on to the clew of thread.

"The ditzy broad is a lousy screw, but the thread trick isn't a bad idea," he thought. "And lining up the boat for a quick getaway isn't too bad either. Now all I have to do is get into the labyrinth, knock off the bull-creep, get out, and sail away for my next big heroic adventure."

The next morning a squad of twenty armed soldiers marched the fourteen Athenians out of their dungeons and to the entrance of the labyrinth. Theseus managed to surreptitiously attach the end of the thread to a knob at the entrance and the contingent was marched a hundred paces into the structure.

The prisoners were shoved, one at a time, into different passageways to wander hopelessly until the minotaur caught and dispatched them.

Theseus managed to place himself at the rear of the group. After all the others had been pushed into the twists and turns devised by Daedalus, it was his turn to be shoved into a passageway. As one of the soldiers reached to push him, the hero grabbed the soldier's sword and dived into the passageway himself.

The soldier had been caught off-guard. But he could not pursue his prisoner to retrieve the sword because he also would then be caught in the maze and subject to the ravages of Prince Minotaurus.

With his newly acquired sword in one hand and the unraveling clew of thread in the other, Theseus wandered as noisily as he could through the mystifying paths. Unlike the others wandering through the elaborate labyrinth, he did not attempt to avoid the monster but to attract it.

Minotaurus was aware that his lunch had been sent into his many-pathed home. He was not only hungry but ready for a bit of sport as well. He heard Theseus clomping around and decided to pursue the noisy human.

As Theseus rounded a turn in the path he encountered the minotaur coming the other way.

Surprise, Minotaurus! A genuine hero with a sword (and a spool of thread) awaits you.

The beast was no match for the great hero, and before he knew it, he was headless.

Carrying the bull-head and the sword, Theseus followed the thread back through the paths he had followed. He gave no thought for his fellow Athenians. If they couldn't find their way back out of the place, tough luck.

When he got back to the entrance, Ariadne was waiting for him. He placed the severed head on the ground as testimony to his heroism.

Ariadne was overjoyed to see him return, and rushed to kiss him.

"Not now, you stupid bitch," he grumbled. "Just get me to the boat and let's get out of here."

The couple made directly for the harbor where a boat with a small crew was awaiting them.

As soon as the escaping couple stepped on deck, the oarsmen set the craft out to sea and at the first stirring of a favorable wind the sails were unfurled.

On the way to Athens the boat stopped at the island of Naxos. While the crew was busy loading the craft with provisions, Theseus and Ariadne were sequestered in a hut on shore that provided shelter for visitors.

During their overnight stay, Theseus remained awake until he was assured that his girlfriend was asleep. He sneaked out of bed and hastened to the ship.

The crew was sleeping on board. Theseus woke them and told them to head out to sea, with him on board and with Ariadne left behind on the small island. He had no intention of being stuck with the silly girl hanging on to him. Heroes have heroic obligations which can only be hampered by starry-eyed clinging broads.

The captain of the ship, loyal to his princess, protested. With one swipe of his sword Theseus beheaded the captain. There were no more protests.

Theseus took on the role of captain and proceeded to reach Athens with the good news that the minotaur was dead. He received in return the information that his father had died while he was off on the Cretan adventure. That also was good news to Theseus. As Aegeus' heir, that made him King Theseus of Athens.

As king, he led his army against the Amazons and won against the women warriors.

Theseus, as king, inherited herds of cattle which were pastured in Marathon.

Pirithous, king of the Lapithae in Thessaly, invaded Attica and prepared to carry off Theseus' herds. Theseus marched to Marathon to repel the invader, leading his troops as general.

As always, Theseus and his men went to battle naked. Pirithous' array was equally unclothed.

When the two armies faced each other, the two generals stepped onto the battlefield to parlay. Theseus took one look at the rugged, handsome features of his adversary and fell in love for the first and only time in his life.

Pirithous saw the lovelight in Theseus' eyes, beheld his beauty and his magnificent cock and balls, and was struck with love as if Cupid's arrow had pierced his heart.

The two swore eternal fidelity to each other and sealed their compact at Theseus' palace back in Athens with wine, kisses, fondling, and deep cornholing, cocksucking and grabass .

It was the beginning of a beautiful friendship.

CHAPTER XIX

ARIADNE GOES WILD

"Boo hoo!"

The Isle of Naxos was flooded with the sounds of Ariadne's sobs.

Her tears, the size of pearls, were flooding the sea.

"That rat! That dirty rat! I gave him my love. I saved his rotten life. He deserted me on this damned island. And, the trouble is, I still love him."

It was the last part of Ariadne's lament that caught Venus' attention. Curses and deprecations of females against the perfidy of males held no interest for the goddess. Male gods and male mortals were a rotten bunch at best. You just have to live with the fact. But a woman who was both sobbing and in love, that was another matter. As the goddess of love, Venus just had to intervene.

Ariadne was not particularly surprised to see the lovely goddess descend from the skies onto the sea and surf a swell of foam onto the shore. She lived in an age of faith and was open to such visitations.

Venus asked the princess what was troubling her and heard the whole sordid story.

"Cease worrying, My Dear," Venus admonished. "I know Theseus, and believe me, he isn't worth a single sob or tear. You have someone worth a thousand Theseuses about to enter your life. Not just some arrogant mortal whose idea of lovemaking is little more than the physical relief of getting his rocks off. The lover for you is nothing less than a god. And not only a god. One of few who really knows how to show a girl a good time."

Well, *that* certainly cheered up the beautiful princess. Things started looking up right away.

She asked who this divine lover might be.

Venus told her.

"His name is Bacchus. He's the newest god on the block. He's Jupiter's youngest son. As a matter of fact, he was gestated within Jupiter's thigh. That's a long story that's not relevant to your condition.

"Once Bacchus was born from the thigh of the king of the gods, he was restless. He wasn't comfortable in Olympus with its old ways and he took off for exotic places seeking a whole new kind of divinity.

"He went as far as India, visiting our cousin gods there. And he traversed Anatolia where he discovered the secret and art of turning the juice of grapes into wine.

"Wine is the basis of the new religion he was fated to bring into the world. He became the god of wine, irrationality, excess, jubilation, and ecstasy."

Ariadne had never before heard of such a god. Indeed, Bacchus was unknown to most mortals at the time. He was earning adherents to his new religion slowly as he taught the mortals living around the Mediterranean the art of viniculture and the beauties of irrationality and excess.

"Naxos just happens to be Bacchus' favorite island," Venus went on. "And he's heading this way right now in his partyboat."

"How will I recognize him?" Ariadne asked.

"Oh, you won't have any trouble there," Venus told her. "Ever since he discovered wine, he always looks slightly drunk."

Since Ariadne, like most mortals at the time, didn't have any idea what intoxication was, that wasn't much help. But she decided to let the matter drop.

Venus bid farewell to the princess and went skidding out to sea on a blanket of foam.

Ariadne waited quite patiently for the arrival of her divine lover.

Ariadne's ears picked up the advent of her promised divine lover before her eyes did. For, before Bacchus' partyboat appeared on the horizon, wild, ecstatic music composed of flute, harp, cymbal, and ululating high-pitched voices harbingered its approach.

When the partyboat approached the shore close enough for Ariadne to see the passengers, her eyes first fell on the young, rather dissolute young individual sprawled on a throne around whom the other passengers were engaged in an orgy.

By far, the majority of the revelers were female. Like everyone aboard they were naked except for the grape-leaves that crowned their brows. They were dancing wildly while chanting shrilly. Each dancer carried a thyrsus, which was composed of a dildo with a vine entwined around the staff. These women were the Bacchantes, females totally committed to the cult of Bacchus. They employed their thyrsi by stimulating themselves and each other erotically.

The remainder of the party was male. There was Silenus, who was Bacchus' constant companion. He was a bald-headed, corpulent, pug-nosed, jovial old man who urged the others on board to cast off any restraints and let themselves go.

Dancing among the Bacchantes, with fully aroused hardons, were the Satyrs. They had bristly hair, pointed ears, small horns growing out of their foreheads, and goat-like tails. Ariadne was to discover that their entire life was devoted to the pursuit of sensual pleasure.

There was a scattering of Centaurs prancing about and providing the opportunity for a bit of bestiality. And the princess could see that the orgy aboard the boat was devoted to drunken, non-stop sexual indulgence.

The partyboat landed and the merry crowd came spilling ashore in high revelry. The sound of the music intensified. The wild dancing became ever more exuberant. The sexual orgy overcame everyone – Bacchantes, Satyrs, and Centaurs.

Everyone, that is, except Bacchus and Silenus.

Finally, when the merry crew were all frolicking on shore, Silenus staggered ashore with a cup of wine in his hand. He approached the astounded Ariadne and offered her the cup.

"My lord, Bacchus, god of wine, exaltation, and sensual pleasure, invites you to partake of this libation and join him on his throne."

Bacchus arose from his throne and beckoned to the princess.

All thoughts and regrets about Theseus flew from Ariadne's thoughts and evaporated.

The god who beckoned to her excited a whole new sensation of what love could mean.

He was gorgeous in a way Theseus was not. His boyish pecker and nuts were the opposite of gross. They were slim and elegant. And his facial features were not fierce and determined but gentle, smiling, and welcoming.

And, as Venus had told her, he looked slightly drunk.

Ariadne took the cup from Silenus' hand. She raised it towards the welcoming god up on deck and sipped. Bacchus raised his cup in her direction then sipped in return.

Silenus led the princess onto the partyboat. Somehow the throne had been replaced by a couch by the time she got there.

Bacchus greeted his lover with a gentle kiss and guided her onto the couch.

Never could Ariadne have ever imagined that lovemaking could be this exhilarating. Bacchus raised her to orgasm often as the troop returned to the ship and the lascivious furor increased surrounding the couple on the couch who became the center of an orgy that transcended all rational bounds.

The ship departed from Naxos and set sail.

Once on the high seas, the orgy came to a conclusion.

On the morrow, Bacchus addressed his crew.

"O revelers and partakers of the joy I bring to the world. Raise your cups to my consort, my true love, and your queen. I place this golden crown on her head in token of her station among you."

Indeed, Ariadne became Bacchus' queen. The love of the god and the princess continued for as long as she lived.

But Ariadne was mortal. And, as it must be for all mortals, the day finally arrived when she died.

Bacchus mourned for Ariadne. He could not prevent her, however, from passing. But he removed the crown from her brow and cast it up into the sky.

As it ascended, the gems turned into stars.

And there, in testimony to a god's love for his mortal lover, the crown remains forever as a gorgeous constellation.

CHAPTER XX

ORPHEUS GOES TO HELL

Calliope, the muse of music and poetry was a companion of King Oeagus of Thrace. Their son, Orpheus, was born with a natural talent along musical and poetic lines.

Apollo enjoyed spending time with the muses. And when he came visiting Calliope he was impressed by Orpheus' obvious talent.

The god brought the boy a gift of a lyre, which his mother taught him to play.

Orpheus was not only a prodigy on his instrument but was a marvel in improvising lyrics and singing them with the sweetest voice in Thrace. Indeed, in all the world.

Apollo became quite fond of the lad, spending an inordinate amount of time accompanying him in duets.

Hour after hour, day after day, indeed for months and years, the god and the mortal filled the meadows, groves, and hillsides with glorious music.

Nothing was immune to the music they played and sang. The wild beasts came to hear in silent rapture. Boys, girls, shepherds, nymphs, even trees and rocks left their stations and approached the enchantment of the music and the poetry.

Apollo was quite catholic in his sexual tastes and he had a taste for Orpheus. And he tasted him and tasted him and tasted him.

When their music attracted the creatures and the beings of the woodlands, Apollo taught his companion how to make love to the members of their audience.

There was a special technique Apollo had acquired of continuing to strum the lyre while engaging in lovemaking with a nymph, a beast, a boy, a rock, a tree...

Orpheus, like Apollo, had quite a predilection for trees. (If you haven't tried it, don't knock it.)

Eventually Apollo, who was somewhat fickle, showed up less frequently in Thrace, pursuing other interests. But he was nevertheless always fond of the young bard.

Orpheus, on his own, continued to fill his land with joyful music and to attract diverse lovers of all kinds by his playing and singing.

Dwelling in Thrace was a lovely nymph by name Eurydice. On a lovely spring morning she chanced to be gathering flowers in a vale when she was enchanted by the sound of beautiful music. She followed the strains and came upon Orpheus who appeared to be seated on a rock whilst plucking his lyre and singing a bucolic lay. At least, he seemed to be sitting on the rock. At least he was engaged with it in some way.

Eurydice's heart went out to the musician-poet. She was struck with love and knew at once she would love him and only him forever and ever.

When Orpheus caught sight of the nymph, it was a case of love at first sight. For this lovely creature he would give up erotic attraction for all other creatures for so long as the nymph should live. He gave up doing whatever he had been doing with the rock, approached Eurydice, clasped her to his bosom and declared his love in song.

And thus the happy couple was wed.

Orpheus was true to his original conviction. He was true and faithful only to his Eurydice. All his songs became love songs directed at his wife. And all Thrace rejoiced in the union of its poet and his love.

However, one spring day, Orpheus was singing and strumming in a sylvan meadow while Eurydice was dancing in joyful abandon nearby but out of sight.

A shepherd by the name of Aristaeus caught sight of the nude dancer and was immediately filled with lust.

Eurydice was aware of the shepherd and his full erection signaled his intent to her.

Fleeing the shepherd, the nymph stepped on a snake that was coiled in the grass. The snake thrust its fangs into her foot, injected its venom, and Eurydice fell dead onto the earth just as Aristaeus caught up with her.

The shepherd, dismayed by what his lust had wrought, slunk back to his flock.

The nymphs were aware of what happened and informed Orpheus of the tragedy.

The bard wept over the body of his bride and expressed his grief by singing threnodies. His doleful songs elicited tears throughout the upper world and even rang up to Olympus. All nature was aggrieved in response to his songs. Gods and men, beasts and trees, rocks and flowers wept.

But the threnodies did not bring back his lover. She simply was no longer to be found in the world of the living. So he determined to seek her in the regions of the dead.

Orpheus traversed the lands of the Hellenes from Thrace to Taenarus (Cape Matapan) to reach the cave which yields access to the netherworld.

He entered the gloomy cave without trepidation for so intent was he in retrieving his lover that he knew no fear. Down and down he trod the treacherous path to the River Styx.

Charon, the ferryman, responded with anger when he spied the form of a mortal approaching. But Orpheus charmed him with his lay and the ferryman transported him over the river to the regions of death.

At the gate to Hades, Cerberus, the three-headed snarling dog was enchanted by the beautiful music and was soon licking the bard's feet before settling down for a comfortable snooze as Orpheus stepped over him and entered the gate to Pluto's realm.

He encountered the Furies who laid down their whips as he strummed and sang.

As he traversed the region where the damned dwelt, the torments ceased as his song filled their space.

At length, he reached the thrones of Pluto and Proserpine. He strummed his lyre and sang to them his plea.

All the shades in Hades gathered around to hear.

"Love is not lost here, for it is known that the two of you were united and are united yet in love. Love and love alone has led me here. All of us are destined to arrive here sooner or later. Eurydice will return here for eternity, and so will I. But within our true allotted time, I beseech you to return her to me. I will not return alone, so if you deny me this I will remain here now with her."

Proserpine could not resist the dulcet lyrics. Nor even could Pluto who wept for the first and the last time ever.

Pluto summoned Eurydice, who was among the newly arrived shades. She came forth, limping on her wounded foot.

Pluto informed Orpheus that he could take her back to the upper world. But he imposed one condition. He could not turn around and look at her until they were both in the upper world in the sun-drenched air.

Orpheus thanked the king and queen and led off for the upper world with his wife following him.

Since Pluto had given them leave, the couple met no hindrances. Cerberus did not growl. Charon ferried them across the Styx. And despite the temptation, Orpheus did not look back to glimpse his wife.

All the way up the gloomy path towards the Taenarus cave Orpheus sang and played.

But as they approached the cave that gave entrance to the upper world Orpheus began to doubt Pluto. He hadn't been able to hear a sound behind him during the upward journey. Perhaps Eurydice was not there after all. His anxiety got the better of him and he turned around to look back to assure himself that Eurydice was really there.

As their eyes met he saw her being borne back to the infernal regions. They attempted to clasp hands only to grab at the foul air of the passage.

Orpheus attempted to retrace his steps to Hades. But Charon was deaf to his entreaties. Orpheus' music could not prevail over the will of Hell.

Despondently, the bard trudged his way back to the upper world and on to Thrace. On the way his songs were even more doleful than before. The hearts of lions and tigers melted in sympathy. The mountains and rocks wept. All nature shed tears. But to no avail.

When he got back to Thrace his music did not change but its effect did. Everyone and everything within range of his lyre and his voice became horny.

But with Eurydice off in the netherworld, Orpheus had resolved to shun womankind. If his lover was no longer among women, he rejected them.

No, he would not give his love to any woman or nymph other than his Eurydice. He would give his love to boys. He would give his love to beasts. Yea, and to trees. He had not made love to a tree since he met Eurydice, so returned to the practice easily.

But even though he would not make love to women, they were still full of lust for him. They were captivated by his songs to dead love and to his dark sad eyes. They desired to comfort him by cuddling his attractive bronzed body.

But he spurned all their advances.

Rebuffed, the women began to hate the musician. But somehow, they could not bring themselves to attack him.

That is, until one day when a group of Bacchantes in a state of frenzy encountered him.

They danced around him. They wailed their Bacchic chants. They tore off his cock and balls. They ripped off his head. His arms and legs were yanked off his torso. The earth was drenched with his blood as the women shrieked, howled, chanted, and raved while they rended his body to shreds in their orgy.

The Bacchantes threw his head into the Hebrus. The river carried it down to the sea and the currents carried it to the island of Lesbos that the poetic tradition might take root there in anticipation of Sappho, the poetess to come.

They threw his lyre into the river. Apollo retrieved it from there and bore it up to the heavens as a constellation.

They tossed his prick and balls into the river, from which they floated to the sea and were born by the currents to the Isle of Cythera where, transformed to a granite monument, they stand to this day on a promontory as a symbol of the power of love.

Orpheus' shade passed for a third time over the Styx where it was united with Eurydice.

And there the couple embrace with all the ardor they knew in the upper world in eternal copulation.

CHAPTER XXI

PYGMALION SHAGS A STATUE

Pygmalion, a Cypriot sculptor unequalled in skill and scope, was turned off towards women. He had repeatedly fallen in love. And every time he entered a love affair, his partner had turned out to be perfidious in one way or another. One broken heart is certainly allowed to any lover. But by the fifth perfidy by a woman to whom he had given his heart, he had had it.

Not that he turned to boys, or to jacking off. Nor did hetaerae, whose favors could be purchased without the risk of love, interest him. He had given up womankind without having replaced the loss with any substitute outlet.

But meanwhile he had been carving a female figure out of purest ivory. The work was life-size, and represented a woman more perfect in form than any mortal woman who had ever lived.

He painted the hair a golden yellow, the eyes a robin blue, the nails, nipples, and lips a subtle pink. With such adornments she appeared so real that one would have to touch the ivory reality to be convinced that she was other than a living, breathing, breathtakingly beautiful woman.

Even Pygmalion traced the statue's enticing curves in order to convince himself that his work of art was not alive.

He doted on his work and was overcome with love for the figure. He kissed the seductive pink lips and imagined not only a response but had the sensation of her soft pink tongue slipping into his mouth. He addressed the statue and ran his hands over its breasts. He reached between her legs and fondled the cold ivory, causing warmth to envelope his nuts.

He brought her gifts and bedecked her with jewels and ornaments.

Pygmalion had fallen hopelessly in love with the work of art he had fashioned himself. He felt he would go mad if he could not consummate his love.

With his tools he drilled a hole where her vagina would have been. Its circumference would comfortably contain his own dick. He crafted a cover for the hole that fit so perfectly that it was invisible to the naked eye.

He laid the statue on his bed covered with blankets of Sidonian coloring. He rested her head on goose-down pillows.

He locked his doors, uncovered his statue, and removed the cover to the convexity he had excavated. He filled the cavity with warm Hymettus honey and made passionate love, denying to himself that the ivory was cold and unresponsive.

On the first day of Spring the great festival of Venus was celebrated throughout the Greco-Roman world. And central to the festival were the ceremonies celebrated on the goddess' favored island of Cypress. Votaries gathered there from every settlement around the Mediterranean Sea.

As a resident of the island, Pygmalion was in attendance.

Choice heifers were sacrificed to the goddess at all of her temples while incense wafted the prayers of the devotees up to Olympus.

Pygmalion brought his offering to the altar of the great Cyprian temple and recited his prayer to the goddess of love in humble tones.

"O kind and gracious Goddess. You possess the power to grant the supplications of your devotees. And when the prayer deals with matters of the heart, you are supreme above all gods and goddesses.

"I pray to you that I might have as my lover..."

He could not bring himself to ask for his ivory statue. So, in place of such a rash prayer he said, "...a woman who resembles my ivory statue."

It will come as no surprise to anyone that Venus herself was physically present at her Great Cyprian Temple on her prime feast day. She understood what Pygmalion's underlying prayer really meant.

The sculptor observed the altar flame intensify three times in acknowledgement that the goddess had heard his supplication.

When he had wended his way back to his home, Pygmalion proceeded directly to the bed whereon his masterpiece lay.

He removed the cover and gazed at his creation. He leaned down and kissed her. Was it his imagination or were those lips actually warm and yielding? He ran his hands over her breasts. The feeling was not that of ivory. In all the world there is no sensation to the male hand that remotely elicits the response of a female breast.

And yet, the sculptor retained doubts about whether a divine metamorphosis had occurred.

He palpated the entire surface of the body. Wonder of wonders, it was real human flesh. He could feel the pulse beating beneath his fingers. He inserted a finger into the vagina. It received the thrust. He held the finger to his nose and then inserted it into his mouth. No question about it. This was no longer an ivory statue with honey in its love tract. It was a living, breathing woman.

Pygmalion raised his hands heavenward and gave praise and thanks to Venus.

He pressed his lips to his creation's once again.

This time the maiden felt the kisses, opened her eyes, and as she caught sight of him, returned the kiss first with gentle suction then with the intrusion with her tongue into Pygmalion's mouth.

The sculptor kissed her body on every surface and inserted his tongue into every crevice and concavity he had previously sculpted.

Venus had endowed the lovely creature with a great talent in the arts of love.

Pygmalion and Galanthis, for such was the lovely creature's name, were deeply in love for so long as they both lived. And Venus granted them the boon that they both die at the same time, enclosed in each other's arms.

CHAPTER XXII

PERSEUS GIVES A FLYING SHAG

Perseus, a great hero of the fabulous age in which he lived, was the son of Jupiter and Princess Danae of Argos.

He was conceived when Jupiter shagged the princess doing a number he called Golden Showers. But, out of decency, the less said about that sordid little operation the better.

Perseus grew up to become a great favorite with many, but not all, of the gods and goddesses of Olympus.

For services rendered, Perseus was given a Gorgon's Head by the goddess Minerva and a pair of winged sandals by the god Mercury.

The Gorgon's Head was the decapitated head of a maiden who had serpents instead of hair on her head. It was Perseus who had decapitated her, but Ovid was not interested in telling that story so it will not be dealt with here. The important point was that anyone who looked at the Gorgon's Head was immediately turned to stone.

The winged sandals were just like Mercury's and enabled Perseus to fly around and hover like a big bird.

Perseus flitted about the Mediterranean basin north, south, east, and west. He had multiple adventures and numerous romantic encounters. His specialty with the ladies was to hover above them, engage in thrilling foreplay with his fine-feathered sandals, then float above them as his hardon glided in and out of their mouths and cunts. He very likely learned the technique from Venus' son Cupid.

Ovid picks up his story on the occasion of Perseus' encounter with Atlas near the Pillars of Hercules. By flashing the Gorgon's Head at the giant he turned him into a mountain.

From there Perseus flew East to Ethiopia in search of further adventure. He had never had occasion to meet black people and was interested in visiting them.

He looked down on Ethiopia as he soared over the land. When he arrived at the Red Sea he spied a gorgeous woman, the color of polished ebony, chained to a rock facing the sea. In his previous romantic encounters he had run into a number of females who favored bondage as their preferred sexual outlet. It seemed clear to the hero that the beauty below was of that inclination.

He descended and hovered above Andromeda, for such was the damsel's name.

She greeted him with an expression of relief. So, hovering above her, he proceeded to give her a right royal fucking.

His technique was borrowed from the god Cupid, who practiced levitated bondage with his sweetheart Psyche.

After satisfying both the beauty and himself, he asked her if she had had enough and why she had chosen that particular spot for bondage.

In reply she told him she was the princess of Ethiopia. Her mother, Cassiopeia, was queen of the land and her father, Cepheus was king.

Her mother had angered the gods who had consequently sent a gigantic sea-monster to ravage the Red Sea coast. King Cepheus had been informed by an oracle that all he had to do to appease the monster was chain his daughter to a rock by the sea so she could be eaten by the monster.

Cepheus did not seem to be overly bothered by the idea, and thus Andromeda was in the condition in which Perseus had found her.

"In such a dire condition," Perseus said to her, "I am surprised you welcomed my attentions."

"In my condition, getting fucked by a gorgeous hunk like you seemed like a welcome diversion. I just hope you can get me out of this mess," she replied.

And, of course, it was the hero's intent to do just exactly that.

While the couple was thus discussing, a roar issued from the sea.

The couple looked out over the waves and saw a giant, vicious monster approaching the shore. Andromeda screamed in her fright. Her parents, who were, after all, responsible for their daughter's plight came down to the shore to wring their hands and offer advice if anyone would ask for it. Being model parents, they beat their breasts and wept copious tears as the monster licked its lips in anticipation of a yummy Andromeda snack.

Perseus approached Cepheus and Cassiopeia and bragged about what a nifty hero he was and how he was going to save their daughter.

All he asked for doing the deed was that they allow their daughter to be his live-in girlfriend after he got rid of the monster. And...oh, yes. They would have to give him a kingdom for his troubles.

The dutiful parents agreed to his terms.

That agreement made, Perseus faced the sea. And sure enough, here came the monster full tilt.

Perseus took off in his winged sandals and jetted up into the clouds.

The sea-serpent saw Perseus' shadow flitting across the waves and attacked it ferociously. The hero swooped down from above while the monster was fighting the shadow. He placed his sword into the roaring sea-serpent's right shoulder the entire length of the curved hook. The monster reared up and then dove down beneath the surface of the sea.

The monster erupted from the depths and burst into the air aimed directly at Perseus. The beast's fangs certainly would have pierced the hero were he not adept with his wings. By means of his mobility Perseus drove his hooked sword time and time again into the sea-serpent's most vulnerable spots.

But look! Perseus' wings are becoming drenched from the monster's violent splashes and writhing. They were cutting down on his maneuverability.

Perseus landed on the very rock where Andromeda was chained.

With the Gorgon Head still clutched in his left hand he directed the object directly at the head of the beast as it rose and lunged towards him. The monster was turned to stone and sank to the bottom of the Red Sea, where its petrified form can be seen to this day by the pearl divers of Ethiopia.

Perseus released the ebony-toned beauty while her father and mother clapped and cheered at the fearless bravado of the winged-shoed hero.

The king, the queen, the princess, and the hero proceeded to the great golden palace where a lavish celebration was held.

Following the celebration, Perseus flew back to Argos bearing his new lover in his arms.

Alas! Perseus could not remain in Argos long while adventures far a-field called for new exploits. There were potentially thousands and thousands of women beyond Argos to the north, south, east, and west who could instruct him in finding new techniques and positions in which to develop his specialty of the flying fuck.

Truth to tell, Andromeda had already grown bored with his constant preoccupation with bondage. She had lost all interest in the practice back on a rock facing the Red Sea.

She saw her lover, of course, when he returned from his constant flights. But in the meantime, she was well treated at the court of Argos where her flighty lover had left her.

And Perseus' father, Jupiter, placed her in the heavens as a constellation after she died. And she remains happy to this day that Perseus has lost interest in her and never flies up into the heavens trying to get her to submit to sexual bondage and his famous flying fuck any more.

CHAPTER XXIII

JASON, HERCULES, AND THE CATAMITE

The god Mercury once gave a flying ram with a golden fleece to Queen Nephele of Aelia, a kingdom in Thessaly. The king sought to murder his twin children so the queen put her son and daughter on the ram and sent them flying off to Colchis, a kingdom far off on the eastern shore of the Black Sea.

As the golden-fleeced ram flew over the Dardanelles, Princess Helle fell off and landed in the water below. That is why the ancients called the strait the Hellespont.

When the ram landed at Colchis, Prince Phrixus was hospitably received by Aeetes and Medea, the king and the princess of the country.

Prince Phrixus sacrificed the ram to Mercury in thanks for his safe voyage and gave the fleece to his host.

King Aeetes hung the fleece in a consecrated grove and protected it with a sleepless dragon.

Meanwhile, back in Thessaly, there was another kingdom near Aelia called Crethea ruled over by King Aeson.

The king was tired of his job and turned the kingship over to his brother Pelias. He stipulated that Pelias could only remain the sovereign until Aeson's son Jason reached the age of eighteen.

Pelias ruled the kingdom quite happily, enjoying the power, prestige, and wealth that pertain to the kingship. And as he watched Jason grow and mature, he plotted how to retain the power when and after his nephew reached his majority.

When Jason came of age and approached his uncle claiming the crown, Pelias was ready for him.

"Quite right, Jason," Pelias smiled. "The crown is rightfully yours for the asking. But a husky, handsome, bright lad like you should not be content to settle down so young. There is adventure, glory, honor, and prestige to be experienced in one's youth.

"Just consider the heroes who inhabit our world – Hercules, Theseus, Orpheus, and Nestor, to name but a few. They have earned their laurels, their renown, and their acclaim by having performed heroic deeds before they were your age. That's what you want to do if your subjects are to respect you. You've got to show that you've got balls."

Jason bought every word his uncle uttered. He felt stirred by the call to adventure. It was true he had done nothing truly heroic heretofore.

Pelias saw by the excitement in Jason's eyes that he had sold the bill of goods. Now, to spring the trap with a specific adventure that Jason would go for.

"Now Jason," Pelias continued. "The family's honor is tarnished by that theft of our Golden Fleece. If you really want to impress our people with your bravery and heroism, I'd suggest that you go to Colchis and get that fleece back from King Aeetes. When you manage that, your fame will outmatch that of Hercules himself."

Jason was husky and handsome, as his uncle had mentioned. But bright? Possibly not so much. Because he never stopped to consider the statement that the Golden Fleece had been stolen from his family. In fact, it had never had anything whatsoever to do with his family or his kingdom.

"You're right, Uncle Pelias," Jason enthused. "I'll go get our Golden Fleece back. I'll collect the greatest heroes living on the shores of the Mediterranean. I'll lead them off on the greatest adventure ever undertaken. No one has yet navigated beyond our sea, through the Hellespont, and on to the farthest reaches of the Black Sea. And to retrieve the Golden Fleece of a ram sent here by Mercury. I'll do it."

"You've got balls, Boy, balls!" Pelias encouraged him. "Go for it."

To which he added, in thought only, "And don't bother ever to come back, Stupid."

Jason began to organize for his big adventure immediately. Uncle Pelias assured him that the entire resources of the kingdom were at his disposal. That meant there was sufficient gold for him to commission the greatest shipwright in the world to build him a vessel capable of carrying as many as fifty men to the farthest reaches man could navigate, namely Colchis.

That craftsman was Argus who came to Thessaly and agreed to build such a boat for the young prince.

The marvelous craft was indeed constructed, and in honor of its builder it was named the Argo.

It was the grandest seagoing vessel ever constructed until that time. Indeed, it was generations before such a challenging shipbuilding task was even considered by any king, prince, or hero again.

The adventure of sailing such a distance in quest of such a prize as the Golden Fleece appealed to the greatest heroes of the Mediterranean world. By the time Argus had completed his task Jason had assembled the greatest crew of stalwart heroes living. There were fifty adventurers including the men Pelias had mentioned – Hercules, Theseus, Orpheus, and Nestor.

The brave crew under Jason's leadership set sail from Crethea with much fanfare. King Pelias waved a hearty farewell from the shore smiling joyously in assurance that the Argonauts would meet a fatal end. How could that musclebound motley crew led by his dimwitted nephew possibly survive such a harebrained voyage?

In two weeks the Argo landed at Mysia to reprovision.

All the Argonauts disembarked to enjoy the freedom of being on land again and to assist with securing provisions.

Not all the passengers on the Argo were heroes or soldiers. Some thirty or so were catamites, boys who provided the same sexual services for their masters that Ganymede provided for Jupiter.

Hercules had brought along a particularly pretty boy named Hylas.

The catamites, though generally less husky than the heroes, were sent on errands during the stay in Mysia. Hylas was sent with a pail to find a spring and bring back some fresh water for the ship's cistern.

While Hylas was searching for a spring, Hercules went hunting for wild game or domestic cattle

Hercules came upon a herd of cattle, rustled an enormous bull, clubbed the animal to death, carried it down to the shore, and butchered it. Five members of the crew were assigned the task of cooking and preserving the meat for the impending voyage to Colchis.

Hercules, like the rest of the Argonauts who had brought their catamites with them, planned to release his sexual tensions while ashore and looked around for Hylas.

No one had seen the lad return to the ship with any water.

Hercules let out a roar of frustration and raged inland in search of his beloved.

He ran wildly over hill, across rill, and onto a meadow. And what he saw in that meadow was a spring.

And beside that spring he espied his lover. And was Hylas ever having himself a time.

There were twelve Naiads, nymphs of that spring, engaged in a veritable orgy. And the center of that sex-fest was Hylas, stretched out on the grass beside the spring.

The Naiads were laving his beautiful body with their tongues and mouths. One was straddling his mouth so he could enjoy cunt eating. There was one on either side of him. His right hand was engaged in pleasuring one's snatch. His left hand was fondling the tits of the other. One of the Naiads was engaged in sucking him off while another was busy licking his balls. Still another managed to get a finger up his asshole.

Somehow, inspired by the boy's beauty, all twelve nymphs were able to do Hylas.

Hercules was enraged.

He charged into the party shouting curses not only at the Naiads, but at Hylas as well.

One would think that a fight between the strongest man in the world and a mere twelve svelte, shapely nymphs would be all over in a matter of seconds. Or minutes at the most.

Not so. The enamored nymphs joined forces and nearly put the strongman to route.

This battle compared in ferocity with his fight with the Nemaean lion, the Lernean Hydra, even with the Amazons. To battle with one woman in love is a gigantic task. To take on a dozen is a travail.

The battle lasted for hours while Hylas dangled his feet in the spring and observed the entertaining battle.

Eventually, one by one, the Naiads dove back into their spring, leaving just Hercules and Hylas on the meadow.

Hercules was fatigued from his battle. But not too tired to engage in an extended bout of sodomy with the lad who was the prize to be won from the battle.

After having buggered him royally, Hercules carried Hylas on his back down to the shore.

When they got to the sea, they discovered that the ship had put to sea. Jason had patiently waited for the strongman and his catamite long enough.

Hercules, with his lover on his back, trudged on foot back to Thessaly.

No one there dared ask him why he had seemingly abandoned the Argo.

CHAPTER XXIV

JASON SHAGS MEDEA

There were several adventures and challenges for the Argonauts as they traversed the Hellespont, sailed past Troy, and entered the Black Sea (which Ovid insists on calling the Euxine). Other poets discuss all that, but since Ovid did not think any of it fit to record in his *Metamorphoses*, I can hardly translate any of it. In the opening lines of Book VII he launches Jason and his Argonauts due eastward across the Black Sea and lands them in Colchis.

King Aeetes himself, accompanied by his lovely daughter Medea, was standing at the shore. As the Argonauts disembarked, the king and the princess greeted each one (including the catamites) with warm embraces.

In conformity with the customs of the time, the Greek warriors wore their crested helmets and their sandals, but naught else.

When Princess Medea got an eyeful of Jason, it induced a heavy case of love at first sight. When she greeted him with the welcoming embrace, she slipped her tongue unobtrusively into his mouth and craftily slid her velvety hand over his scrotum.

Jason was *very* aware of the princess and was happy to discover how very hospitable these barbarian people seemed to be.

King Aeetes had his chamberlain install the visitors in separate rooms in his lavish palace. That is, except those heroes who had brought along their lovers. The Colchians knew better than to separate master from catamite.

A splendid banquet was served that evening in the great hall to honor the guests.

At the banquet, Jason informed the king that he had traveled the unprecedented distance by ship for the express purpose of acquiring the Golden Fleece in order to return it to Thessaly.

The Colchian king was as wily as Jason's Uncle Pelias. Rather than resisting the brash demand, he pretended to agree outright.

"Of course," he responded. "After such an arduous journey, you certainly deserve the Golden Fleece. You need not have brought all your brave warriors with you to wrest the fleece from us. It is yours."

Jason was nearly disappointed that he and his heroic companions would not have a chance to win a glorious battle against the barbarian Colchians. But now that King Aeetes had shown himself so hospitable he was forced to show how civilized he was and thanked his host profusely.

"There's just one thing, Prince Jason, that I feel I must tell you," the king continued. "The great god Mercury established a requirement concerning the removal of the Golden Fleece from its consecrated grove."

Of course, Mercury had not given a thought to the fleece one way or another. But Jason was as gullible in Colchis as he had been back in Thessaly. So he swallowed Aeetes' deceitful explanation without question.

Wide eyed, he inquired what that requirement might be.

"The person removing it must prove himself sufficiently brave and heroic by performing two insignificant feats."

Now this was more up Jason's alley. The feats might be 'insignificant.' But they were considered demonstrations of bravery and heroism. That was really what he had set sail for originally. He asked what was involved.

"In the Field of Mars just outside our city there is a pair of fire-breathing bulls who have brazen hooves. All the hero has to do is yoke them to a plough and sow the teeth of the dragon Cadmus slew here some while back.

"There's one curious little wrinkle Mercury added. When the dragon teeth are ploughed into the earth a crop of armed warriors springs up and they turn their weapons on the hero."

That was just the kind of challenge Jason relished. He would need to plan a strategy of course. He would work something out after dinner.

He was now free to ogle the princess who had greeted him so fondly on his arrival to the kingdom.

He glanced at Medea. She returned his look and ran her tongue around her lips in a lascivious manner. Jason felt a tingly sensation in his nuts. He recognized the feeling as the precursor to a boner.

One of the disadvantages of going around in the Greek tradition, that is to say bare-ass naked, is that it is painfully difficult to conceal your hardons.

So as not to embarrass himself at the state banquet, he had to rapidly look away and think of something besides the princess' ample hooters and fetching beaver.

He thought about how boring most of the voyage had been and quieted the near social disaster.

Medea had noted the quiver of the hero's dick and grew moist in her gasping cunt.

Jason could not resist glancing back at the princess. She repeated her tongue maneuver. Another testicular twinge. Another reverie about the dullness of crossing the vast seas. A new infusion of dampness from Medea's vagina.

The incidents continued ceaselessly for the rest of the dinner. It turned out to be a banquet that seemed interminable.

At length Jason and his Argonauts thanked the king and princess for a delightful banquet and took their leave to return to their chambers.

Jason, relieved that he got through is gonadal challenge without disgracing himself, returned to his room knowing without question that Princess Medea would soon be meeting him for a jolly romp.

That walk was painfully joyful. The ache in his balls from the suppression of his erection had actually hampered his walking ability. The pleasure of anticipation of the undoubted erotic encounter to come with Medea compensated for the physical pain in his nuts.

Once back in his room, he was fidgety as he anticipated a knock on his door.

There was no knock. After a short wait, Medea entered his room without a knock. She entered wearing a diaphanous robe which she discarded upon entering. The rapid disrobing coincided exactly with the sprouting of Jason's erection.

Medea took him aggressively by the hand and led him through the large livingroom and directly to the enormous couch in the boudoir.

The princess was quite aware of Jason's need to relieve the pain from his extended suspension of his priapic tendencies during the banquet. As a result, she guided his quivering prick directly into her love channel as soon as they hit the couch.

After their rapid climax, they lay contentedly in each other's arms.

When Jason had recuperated sufficiently for the next bout of fucking, Medea unleashed her secret sexual weapon. Both participants, after having achieved the first desperate climax, were ready for a long, languid session of foreplay including visual, olfactory, tactile, and gustatory erotic excursions.

When they jointly came to the crescendo of foreplay into a wild fuck, Jason made his phallic entry into Medea's garden of delights. What he experienced several moments before his orgasm was the sensation of an entity that apparently descended from deep within his lover's womb, that encircled his peckerhead and with a delicious moist warmth sucked the jism from somewhere deep within his body deep into her pneumatic uterus.

Medea, it must be told, was a priestess of Hecate, the three-headed goddess of the occult. In the vernacular, that meant Medea was a witch, or a sorceress. And as such she was given the gift of anguism, the sucking serpent that descends from some mysterious location well beyond the cervix precisely when the pecker is primed to come.

Jason had had sufficient erotic experience with both males and females when he was younger to have thought he knew most of what there was to know about the *ars amatoria*. But the experience of anguism surpassed any and every sexual rapture he had explored or even imagined.

He was exhausted, panting, and in a state of absolute delight.

He was left in a state of passion for his bedmate that caused Medea to believe the hero was completely devoted to her. She intended to get this love of her life to marry her and take her back to Thessaly where she would be his queen and the mother of his children.

Now, it was imperative that she prevent him from being killed on the morrow in his encounter with the fire-breathing bulls, the children of the dragon's teeth, and a contest of which he had not yet been informed, a sleepless dragon.

CHAPTER XXV

JASON AND THE EVIL GODDESS

As they were basking in sweet dalliance, Medea asked Jason if he had a strategy devised for dealing with the bulls and the dragon-teeth warriors.

"Not yet," he admitted. "I'm working on it. But I've been kind of busy since your father informed me of the labors Mercury imposed on the action."

"There is only one way the labors can be performed with guaranteed success," she informed him. "But you need to know there are not two labors involved, but three. My father did not reveal the third one."

Jason of course was interested in hearing about the third task ahead.

"There is a dragon guarding the consecrated grove within which the fleece has been placed," she informed him. "The dragon never sleeps. To get past him and retrieve the fleece, you need to lull the beast to sleep. Once it dozes, all you have to do is enter the grove, bundle up the fleece, and walk right past the dragon while it's still asleep."

That seemed like a paltry kind of adventure for a great hero like himself. All he would have to find out was how to put the sleepless dragon to sleep.

"You say you have a strategy for all this?" he asked his couch mate. "Would you care to share it with me so I can take it under consideration?"

Medea told him that she did, indeed, have a fool-proof system for solving the problems involved in all three tasks. But that she was bound by her vows to Hecate to reveal it only to her husband.

Husband?

Yes, husband.

Jason mulled over in his mind what it would be like to be married to this woman. He decided that to be married to a beautiful, voluptuous woman who could and would give him anguism was a most pleasing prospect. But he wanted to up the ante somewhat to trade his bachelorhood for a promised strategy.

"Do you have any other little tricks in store for a husband? That anguism is terrific. But..."

Medea understood, and even expected this buff, gorgeous Greek to bargain a bit.

She replied, "I have so many techniques that you can enjoy a fresh thrill every night for as long as we are married. Would you like to sample another?"

He did.

She had brought along a love philter just for such a contingency. She mixed the philtre into the amphora of wine that had been placed in his room and poured the mixture into his goblet. He drank the concoction and settled back. He felt a current surge through is body as his lover sucked his cock while running a gentle finger up his ass, messaging his prostate gland. His orgasm was immediate.

With his cum in her mouth, Medea kissed her future husband. As the jism passed into his mouth he had an actual oral orgasm.

Jason never imagined such ecstasy was possible.

He begged her to marry him.

Medea had accomplished her mission.

When Jason had gotten over the divine delirium occasioned by his oral orgasm, Medea whisked him directly to the Grove of Hecate so they could be married by the goddess herself.

Ovid felt no need to tell his first century readers who and what Hecate was. But for the readers of this, my translation, I feel the need to explain a word or two about this mysterious goddess.

When Jupiter and his Olympians defeated the old gods, the Titans, he sent them to Tartarus, a place as far below Hades as the heavens are above the earth. An iron gate keeps them imprisoned there forever. Hecate was a Titan, and the only one not sent to Tartarus. Her occult powers were such that not even the ruling, triumphant Olympians dared send her there.

She summoned the shades from Hades and haunted the earth with them at will. She was the mistress of magic, sorcery and witchcraft.

Not even the gods mentioned her by name unless it was absolutely necessary. Her priestesses, devotees, and witches could, however, address her by name. The ancients called her by the term Triceps, the three headed one, to void summoning her with her awesome and evil power.

It was by that name that Medea mentioned her to Jason.

Medea led a dog on a leash with her as she conducted Jason to the shadowy grove. She asked Jason to carry his sword along to the ceremony.

She warned Jason not to look at the goddess. Even her devotees quake at the sight. Those who have not been bound to her by solemn oath seldom recover from the shock of beholding the three-headed one.

The lovers stared at each other in the grove. The priestess, Medea, as she chanted a hymn to her goddess placed the dog on the marble altar that stood in the center of the wickedly holy spot.

The dog whined a frightened, mournful whimper that served as a complement to Medea's chant.

Medea took Jason's sword from his hand, raised it above the canine's whine, and with one swift blow beheaded the sacrificial offering.

As the dog's blood flowed over the altar, Jason was aware of a presence that appeared suddenly behind the altar. He felt surrounded by a force so evil it made him shudder. He kept his eyes steadily focused on Medea's breasts.

A sepulchral voice asked him whether he agreed to join the priestess in sanctified wedlock. He muttered that such was his wish. A similar question was asked of Medea. She agreed.

He felt the presence of shades from Hades surrounding the ceremony as witnesses. They emitted a low, moaning sound.

The goddess demanded that a coupling be performed before the two could be declared man and wife.

Medea lay down on the grassy turf, disrobed, and spread her legs. It was clear to Jason what he was supposed to do. He frankly wondered whether he would be able to perform the sacred penetration.

As he knelt between his bride's outspread, welcoming legs, her hands fondled his cock and balls into the required hardon, and he emptied his seed into her womb.

The evil goddess placed a packet of charmed herbs and a magic amulet upon the altar. Medea was well schooled in their use.

At the moment of his ejaculation, the evil creature behind the altar disappeared along with the witnessing shades.

Jason and Medea were husband and wife.

CHAPTER XXVI

JASON THROWS THE BULL

The next morning, when the twinkling stars had been extinguished by rosy fingered dawn, the crowds had already assembled at the Field of Mars.

Sitting in the stands, surrounded by the crowd, sat King Aeetes, wearing his purple cape and bearing his ivory scepter. On one side of the field sat the Colchians and on the other the Argonauts.

In the center of the field were the yokes, the harnesses and the plow.

Onto the field charged the brazen-footed bulls breathing fire. Striding forth onto the field from the other side was Jason, chief of the Argonauts, with his sword in hand, his helmet shining on his head, his sandals on his feet, and a packet of enchanted herbs and a magic amulet in a pouch attached to a golden belt that circled his naked waist.

The beasts facing him pawed the earth with their brass hooves and bellowed fiercely. As they set themselves to charge the hero, he approached them. The Colchians were astounded. The Argonauts shouted their encouragement. And Jason, a packet of the herbs filling his right hand while holding his sword in his other, reached the beasts just as they were ready to charge, stepped deftly to the side as they charged past him, and sprinkled them with Hecate's herbs.

The bulls turned about and quietly plodded towards Jason. Jason placed a yokes around their necks and drove them to draw the plow to cut furrows into the field.

That task accomplished, from his pouch the hero took the dragon's teeth the king had given him and cast them into the furrows the bulls had created.

No sooner did the teeth fall into the earth than the forms of armed men sprouted from them.

When the Greeks saw the warriors aiming their spears at the broad naked breast of their Thessalian leader, they were sore afraid. And even the hero's bride, assured that the amulet he carried would save him, had moments of fear and alarm. One lone hero confronted with a host of foes was enough to cause his champions to tremble and grow pale.

Jason hurled the magic amulet into the midst of his foes, which turned their hostility away from him towards each other. A furious battle raged until every member was exterminated.

Now Jason's remaining task was to put to sleep the sleepless dragon.

Jason approached the consecrated grove and sprinkled the monster with the required herb. With the recitation of the words Medea had taught him, the eyes that had never before slept closed in gentle slumber.

The crew of the Argo was directed to hasten to the harbor, board ship, and prepare to sail as soon as their captain boarded.

Jason grabbed the Golden Fleece and joined by his bride reached the ship while King Aeetes and his subjects were too dumbfounded by the proceedings to be aware of what was happening.

The Argonauts, their chief, and the Colchian princess set sail and were well out of range of Aeetes and his warship while confusion reigned in Colchis.

CHAPTER XXVII

SEXUAL FRUSTRATION ABOARD
THE ARGO

King Aeetes' warship was much smaller than the Argo, and thus was manned by a smaller crew. But because it was much lighter than the famed Argo, it was capable of moving somewhat swifter.

Medea spied the approach of her father's ship, and was determined that she and Jason should not be overtaken.

The evil procedures she ployed are recorded by many of the ancient writers. But Ovid was so revolted by her tactics that he refused to set them to his divine verses.

I will follow the great poet's lead and leave the sorceress' vile actions be. Suffice it to say that Aeetes turned his warship back to Colchis in disgust and the Argo proceeded on towards Thessaly without further pursuit.

Which does not mean that the return voyage carried a uniformly happy crew.

As any captain of an all-male crew knows, at the outset of a voyage, his crew is in good spirits. On the long trip back home, it is another matter.

When the great adventurer sets out, discomforts are at a minimum.

However, after weeks or months at sea, what at first seemed minimal malaise becomes a major annoyance. And when the resulting annoyance causes disgruntlement among a group of crewmembers, the situation can lead to real trouble for the captain.

Jason himself was in a state of great satisfaction and happiness. Medea had promised him a different sexual delight, or a sequence of erotic satisfactions, every day they would be on board.

And many of his crew members were pleased and satisfied with the provision for their sensual cravings and needs. But some felt acute distress in their gonads on the return trip. And that problem group was, of course, the venusians.

Let us consider first, though, the sailor-warriors who posed no libidinal problems for their leader.

There was, of course, a merry group of pedophiles. They had brought their catamites along with them and suffered no sexual deprivation aboard either on the voyage to Colchis or on the return trip to Thessaly.

Then there were the narcissists. They could not and would not engage with any other person or thing other than their own precious selves. As long as such a one possessed a fist, there was a host of masturbatory options available to him. No matter where the narcissist found himself, he was never lonely for a partner.

Another segment of the crew was made up of the onanists. As long as there were two or more of them to form a daisy chain, they could always engage in a circle-jerk to engage in mutual masturbation. All of the Myrmidons on board practiced this form of relief back when they were in Thessaly. So there was no unhappiness on their part while aboard the Argo. They were a small Achaean race much described in the Iliad. Ovid pretty much leaves them to Homer to describe.

Another happy group among the crew was the sodomites. This was the most promiscuous group of all. Whether in couples or threesomes, there was pleasure aplenty to be had. It was always party time in the quarters of the sodomites.

Which left the unhappy venusians. This was the group on every long voyage that turned out to be the troublemakers. Without any venusians aboard there were not likely to be any mutinous grumbles.

Jason himself was a venusian, of course. But with his enthusiastically sexual partner, namely his wife, keeping him stimulated as often during the day as he was capable of performing, he was among the most content of the forty occupants of the ship.

The curse of the venusians who are aboard a vessel in which there is no female available for the joys of sex, is discomfort, pain, depression, and anger.

For a venusian cannot and will not relieve himself sexually with any creature other than a sexually active female. They are straight.

Jason discussed with Medea what might be done to keep his venusian crew members from becoming a problem.

Medea informed him that she could charm mermaids aboard.

Jason considered the possibilities but concluded that although he knew the creatures to have beautiful faces, breasts, and torsos, he did not believe the other venusians would be any more inclined to engage in shagging the fishy lower half of a mermaid any more than he would.

Medea was inclined to agree.

"The sirens might serve the purposes of your venusians shipmates," she suggested.

The downside of luring the sirens was pointed out to her by her husband.

"Sirens, I know, are nymphomaniacs and, if we could lure some aboard, they would service our heroes splendidly. But they live on their island singing their meretricious chants to the sailors who pass by. No venusian sailor hearing their call can resist throwing himself overboard and swimming to them. Once there, he becomes so enchanted with the variety of sexual favors he enjoys that no mortal can ever get him away from the island.

"I would lose every venusian aboard if we got close enough to a siren island to allow any of my heroic venusians to hear the siren song."

In ancient times the island of Cinara was more noted for its sirens than for its artichokes and was avoided by sea captains.

"Head for Cinara," Medea told him. "I can get a few sirens aboard and I guarantee you will lose no venusians aboard when we get within earshot of the island."

Jason knew that his bride knew her way around such matters and set sail towards Cinara.

Medea called upon Orpheus, a crew member and the most skilled musician who lived, to discuss the strategy with her. Orpheus had been truly omnisexual, luring women, men, girls, boys, trees, wild beasts, and even plant life to him with his irresistible singing and lyre playing. There were few shaggable creatures or objects with whom Orpheus had not engaged in a fuckfest. (That is, before he met Eurydice. But that is a different tale altogether.)

The ploy was for Orpheus to sing and play his most amorous songs as the Argo approached the island. His playing would not only drown out the sirens' songs from the ears of the crew members. It would lure sirens from their island onto the ship. Once on board, the ship would sail away retaining the nymphomaniac nymphs in the arms of the sex-starved venusians.

After the sirens had been lured aboard, every crew member was in fine fettle as the ship ploughed its way back to Thessaly.

On arrival, the Argonauts set out each for his own city touting his renown for being a hero in the latest great adventure.

Jason gave the Golden Fleece to his Uncle Pelias who, disappointed that his nephew had survived the voyage, yielded the crown to him.

King Jason and Queen Medea lived happily in the palace for a while. The main problems Jason now faced were two in number.

First, Medea's sorcery visited myriad ills upon the kingdom. And second, he began to get wearier every day from the exhaustion of the vigorous sexual performances required to enjoy the raptures of Medea's ministrations.

The marriage lasted somewhat over two years. Medea bore Jason two children.

Jason finally had had enough of his witch wife and secretly proposed to Creusa, the royal princess of Corinth.

When Medusa slit the throat of Uncle Pelias and poured foul potions though his veins, Jason knew he could delay no longer.

Medea was aware of his intent, sent a poisoned robe to Creusa, murdered her and Jason's two children, set the palace on fire, got into her chariot pulled by two dragons, and flew off to Athens.

Once there, she married King Aegeus, and on Theseus' return from his Minotaur adventure she attempted to poison him.

She failed in her attempt to poison Theseus. And Creusa never wore the poisoned robe. Medusa seldom missed when doing her sorcery. She was nearly perfect, but not entirely.

When her treachery in Athens was detected, she flew off to Asia where a country called Media thereafter bore an approximation to her name. She lived out a happy evil life there.

Jason and Theseus went on to blaze new adventures.

CHAPTER XXVIII

HERCULES:
STRONGMAN/TRANSVESTITE

Hercules was the son of Jupiter and Alcmena and was thus part immortal from his father's side and mortal from his mother's.

The devious way Jupiter got into Alcmena's bed by taking on the form of her husband while said husband was away on business will not be dealt with in this book.

Hercules' stepmother, Juno, was hostile towards the hero, as she was towards all of Jupiter's whelps by mortal mothers. But she was particularly vicious towards Hercules and repeatedly sought to destroy him.

Hercules grew up to be the strongest, most bulgingly muscular person on earth. And, like his father, he was omnisexual.

His famous twelve labors are described elsewhere. His aborted voyage with the Argonauts is discussed in Chapter Twenty-three above.

At this point in the *Metamorphoses*, Ovid skips to the final years of the mortal period of Hercules' life on earth.

As mentioned, Hercules was omnisexual. But not as the term applies to Jupiter and Orpheus. Unlike them, Hercules had no sexual interest in inanimate objects like rocks and trees and did not turn himself into animals like swans and bulls to do a kind of reverse bestiality. In fact, he had only attempted bestiality once, and that was with a lioness. Neither he nor the cat particularly enjoyed the experience.

But his experience with women, men, girls, boys, nymphs, and satyrs gave him pleasure. Because he was not always aware of his own strength, some of his partners avoided him if they had reason to suspect he was feeling horny.

His final exploit (non-sexual) involved a voyage to Hades where he ran into a former lover, Theseus. He had known Theseus back when they were both on the Argo. But they weren't lovers at that time because Hercules had his catamite with him on the trip. He managed to bring the ex-boyfriend back to earth from Hades on this current adventure. There is no record whether the two got it on either in Hades or when they got back up to earth.

Back on earth when Orpheus had headed back to Thrace, Hercules succumbed to one of his frequent fits of madness and killed his current boyfriend, Iphitus, who was also one of his companions on the Argus years before.

Hercules was tried in the tribunal of Lydia for the murder and was condemned to serve as a slave to Queen Omphale for three years.

The queen was a lesbian with an acute sense of humor. This occurred much, much before the poetess Sappho lived in Lesbos. But even during Hercules' time the practice of sweet love among women on the island was well enough known to have introduced the noun and adjective 'lesbian' into a term signifying the mellifluous intercourse of feminine love.

The queen garbed her newly acquired slave in a long diaphanous, sleeved, lavender gown. Since purple was a decidedly male color, a washed-out purple, or lavender, implied reduced manhood. The garment fit tight over his chest so that his powerful pectoral muscles appeared like breasts through the garment. The sleeves hid his muscular arms and the floor-length robe covered his strong, manly legs.

He did not even resist shaving off his robust beard. When he saw the result in the mirror he laughed so explosively that the very walls shook.

He was assigned to live in the women slave quarters. And he was required to respond daintily when called Herculea.

Hercules had previously experienced every form of lovemaking he had heard of except transvestism. He looked forward to three years of the practice with good humor. The most difficult part of his coming three years of servitude would be to keep the queen from discovering that he was actually enjoying his 'punishment.'

His companions in the slave quarters were all lesbians, of course. Queen Omphale would never have acquired any female slaves with a different bent.

Herculea early figured out how to participate in the orgies that took place in the quarters. By keeping on his attire, thus hiding his masculinity somewhat, he used tongue, lips, and fingers sufficiently graciously to be allowed to participate.

One of the slavegirls was secretly bisexual and enjoyed giving the buff transvestite the relief he needed by performing fellatio on him when the two had a chance to hide from the others in a convenient closet.

The queen sent him once a week to serve in the Lydian hetaerium as a common whore.

Many men visited the Lydian hetaerium to purchase love. But few there were who opted to take to couch one who was not pretty, but, instead, handsome. One who though not petite and dainty, was, instead enormous and robust.

Each of the customers who chose Herculea was in for quite a surprise. As he caressed the bulging breasts, he discovered they were not only firm but as hard as rocks. As he ran his hands up the legs under the lavender robe, they were not daintily shapely and smooth, but muscular and hairy. And on the next groping up to the crotch, he found himself with a handful of cock and balls that always elicited a gasp, then a gulp, and finally a loud exclamation.

As it turned out, no man who had chosen for a couch companion a being as massive as Herculea, with a visage more handsome than beautiful, was ever found to request a refund. As a matter of fact, Herculea had a raft of return customers throughout her three years of servitude.

As a further humiliation, Queen Omphale ordered her slave to sit many an afternoon in the public gardens of Lydia. And despite Herculea's obvious size and physiognomy, she almost always attracted at least one sporting man who hoped to grab at least a good feel from the handsome beauty.

Not a one of these left without propositioning the one with the surprising assets.

At the end of the three year servitude, Hercules returned the lavender garb to the queen and set off for Thessaly and the Oeta mountains.

He dwelt in the mountains for three years. At the end of the three years he felt death's approach.

He climbed to the peak of Mount Oeta, constructed a funeral pyre for himself, and lay atop it. He rested his head on his club and wrapped his lion skin around him.

He set the pyre aflame and with calm countenance he was consumed.

The flames could only destroy those parts of him he inherited from his mortal mother. What he had inherited from his father, Jupiter, could not be destroyed.

That part of him that was divine was transported to Olympus where he was welcomed by all the gods except Juno.

Of all the gods, it was Hebe the cupbearer who was immediately infatuated with him.

Juno, who realized she would have to accept him, married Hercules to her daughter Hebe.

Hercules, though not in love with Hebe, married her gladly. For he knew he would be no more faithful to her than his father would ever be to Juno.

And he knew it was very unlikely that he would ever wear a lavender robe in Olympus. He had tried transvestism. It had been lots of fun. But he decided other forms of sexuality suited him better.

And what happened to the Golden Fleece?

No one since its return to Greece seems to know or care.

CHAPTER XXIX

ATALANTA FALLS FOR AN APPLE

Atalanta was a tomboy. Her face had a boyish cast, so she was referred to as handsome rather than beautiful. But all thought her very attractive indeed.

Her body was fit and firm, with breasts smallish, firm, and eminently perky and admirable.

She was a perfect athlete, who had smooth, lovely musculature.

She could out throw any youth in Boeotia with the discus. She could have out wrestled any youth, but did not wrestle after puberty since the lads could not engage her in the sport without springing a hardon. And a wrestling match between boy and girl with erection presents a very real advertent or inadvertent chance of penetration. And even beyond that, wrestling does not lend itself well to being a priapic sport.

But of all her athletic abilities, none surpassed foot racing. She was known even beyond Boeotia as unbeatable in any running contest.

Atalanta was very interested in boys. She fantasized constantly over every kind of erotic practice possible with all the contemporary lads she knew, or even just happened to see. When she spied a handsome, well muscled youth with an attractive penis, her crotch exuded a warm, honeyed moistness. And since the custom in Boeotia was for the youths to be attired in sandals alone up to the age of 25, she found herself moist much of the time.

When she approached the age of sexual maturity, she inquired of the oracle as to what manner of spouse would suit her best.

The oracle responded with severity.

"O Atalanta, you should never marry. Intercourse with a male will be your bane. However, even knowing this you will surely succumb."

The maid was terrified by this dire prophesy. And so, although intrigued by males, and imagining the delights not only of coitus, delighted in imagining the joys of cunnilingus, fellatio, mutual masturbation, and even sodomy, she repulsed all propositions and proposals.

As she fantasized about frolics with males, she contented herself with masturbation. When invited by maids, she participated in all the Sapphic entertainments known to sexually active girls. And though enjoying them, still got much more excited as she considered the possibilities of sex with boys.

Despite the fact that she could out-do all the boys, she remained extremely popular. She was good looking, witty, healthy, and an intact virgin ripe for fucking.

There was not a heterosexual young man in all Boeotia who did not yearn to shag Atalanta.

So to ward off those who would proposition her, she let it be known that she was available for romantic engagements. She set up one simple condition.

"Come on, boys. I'm ready for any one of you who can beat me in a footrace over a distance of two parasangs. If you win, your prick may penetrate me whenever and wherever you like."

"But what?" she was asked by any lad who considered racing the winsome lassie who made this offer, "if I lose the race?"

"You must agree before the race starts that if you lose to me, you will pay the penalty of being emasculated."

"You mean...?"

"I mean that I will personally cut off your cock and balls with this very knife.'

She exhibited the knife.

Many a young man declined to risk his manhood for a chance to compete for Atalanta's favors.

But there were those who were so smitten by her charms that they signed up to enter the race. As a matter of fact, it was a crowded field.

A circular course was established with a distance from start to finish of two parasangs.

Bleachers were set up and a large crowd of spectators filled them to overflowing.

A young man from Thebes, Hippomenes by name, who had never seen Atalanta, had heard of this cruel race and came to the Asopus Valley, where the contest was to be held. He came simply out of idle curiosity.

He found a seat in the stands and asked a rhetorical question to one of the other spectators:

"What kind of idiot would risk his cock and balls just for a chance to shag some girl? I don't care if she's the most beautiful wench in Boeotia. You wouldn't catch me out there with louts who are warming up for the race."

The words had scarcely passed his lips than Atalanta, naked even to the extent of not wearing sandals, appeared at the starting line.

"Oh, ye gods," Hippomenes exclaimed. "I swear I did not know what the prize was. I am the one who is the idiot."

The official at the starting line gave the signal, and the race was on.

Atalanta's running caused her to appear even more beautiful than she appeared at the start of the race.

There was a crowd of contestants at the race's start. But as Atalanta could be seen rounding the final turn, she was followed by only two youths. It was clear that all the rest of the runners had dropped out of the race along the way and had sneaked off into the woods. They apparently cared more about continuing to preserve their cock and balls than being emasculated finishers. They must have kept running for quite a distance because not a one ever showed his face in Boeotia again.

Atalanta crossed the finish line well ahead of the two intrepid boys who came in second and third.

As Atalanta relieved the two losers of their gonads, the crowd of spectators' groans drowned out the cries of the two unfortunates as Atalanta deftly applied her razor-sharp blade to her competitors' pride and joy.

Hippomenes' infatuation with the fleet-footed girl now overwhelmed him. He strode down to the track to challenge Atalanta even as she was wiping the blood off her sword.

"Beating that field of sluggards, fair nymph, was an unworthy challenge," he proclaimed.

"I love you dearly, and would compete with you at this place and at this time on the morrow. I am the great-great grandson of Neptune, the god of the seas. And I am mightily fleet of foot. If you can defeat me you will indeed have great renown. For Hippomenes is truly a worthy opponent."

Atalanta looked the youth over from head to toe. She liked what she saw. And was even torn between whether she wished to win or lose such a race.

One thing she felt loath to do. And that was to remove from him his most loveable features. Because now, for the first time in her life, she felt love rather than lust.

(But lust was certainly there, too.)

There was no way the maid could refuse to race the Theban with the handsome face, imposing body, and intriguing hanging parts.

Hippomenes retired to a quiet place on a mountainside that appeared to be a site holy to Venus.

He called out a prayer to the goddess of love and a sympathetic breeze carried his prayer to her. She appeared to him with three golden apples. He learned from her how to employ them.

The next day the stands were full to overflowing. And the spectators were rooting for Hippomenes with one accord.

They were surprised to see him carrying three golden apples to the starting line. But they attributed his action to perhaps just some weird Theban thing.

The signal was given and the race was on.

Atalanta, deep in her heart, wanted to slow down and let he youth pass her. But in honesty she could not make herself do it.

Once out of sight of the crowd, Neptune's scion tossed one of the apples ahead where his love caught sight of it.

Venus loved a lover and knew the two runners were in love. She had enchanted that apple to cause Atalanta to have an overpowering wish to engage in one of her erotic fantasies.

Atalanta followed the rolling apple off the course and into the adjacent woods. As Atalanta pursued the apple, Hippomenes followed Atalanta.

The previous evening, as she lay on her couch, Atalanta had envisioned the sheer rapture of the brawny youth comforting her perfumed loins with avid mouth. So now, in this hiatus from the race, she yearned for fulfillment of her fantasy.

As Hippomenes followed the course of the apple and the maiden, he caught sight of her lying on her back, naked, upon the soft earth, apple in hand, legs spread, and knees raised.

The boy knelt between her outspread, welcoming thighs and lowered lips and tongue to her fragrant welcoming snatch.

As Atalanta sighed her welcome to her lover's gentle laving of her twat, Hippomenes brought her to a rapturous climax.

Before he could mange to arise from his sprawled out position, Atalanta had sprung up and had resumed her pace on the track.

Hippomenes scrambled up and set up his former pace behind the maiden's fleeing form.

He was not able to catch up with her, so he tossed the second apple over her head and into the sylvan growth that abutted the track.

Atalanta followed the apple's trajectory and retrieved the golden fruit. As she picked it up a quickening within her womb recalled her waking dream of the previous night in which he lavished her erotic attention on the alluring prick of the gorgeous Theban.

She knelt on the ground as Hippomenes approached her. Without so much as a word from either of them, he was aware of her desire to taste him. He stopped before her, took her head in his hands, and directed her lips to his pecker.

Atalanta fulfilled her desire to fellate the boy of her dreams.

Having swallowed his cum, the girl sprinted back to the course and was on her fleet way again with her lover in blissful pursuit.

Before the turn in the circular track that would bring the racing couple back into sight of the spectators, Hippomenes cast the final apple.

Each of the contestants knew what Venus' intentions were if Atalanta were to retrieve the golden object. When she swerved from the course into the woods, Hippomenes envisioned exactly what he would find when he sped into the glade.

Atalanta was lying on her back on the mossy surface of the earth. That she was receptive to his ardor there could be no doubt.

As the handsome youth entered Atalanta's cunt and ruptured Hymen's shield, Venus, the goddess of love, smiled her loveliest smile.

As the lovers strolled back to the track, Cupid retrieved the golden apples and returned them to his mother.

The spectators cheered as they caught sight of the couple loping down toward the finish line.

Still holding hands, Hippomenes' left foot traversed the finish line a bare second before his lover's.

But the gods, looking down from Olympus declared that it was Love that won the race that day.

CHAPTER XXX

CEPHALUS SHOOTS THE BREEZE

Cephalus was a handsome young man who loved all the manly sports. And he was particularly fond of the hunt. With his hunting dog Lelaps, he pursued all manner of game. But fox hunting was his absolute passion.

He was married to a beauty by the name of Procris.

If Procris had a chief fault it was suspicion. And following close behind suspicion lurked jealousy. And Procris was indeed obsessed by those twin enemies of marital felicity.

By conventional standards, early in their marriage, it could be said that Cephalus was unfaithful to his wife. For he regularly arose before dawn while his wife was still asleep. He left their cottage with bow and arrow on occasion and armed with his spear on others. And accompanied by Lelops, Cephalus went into the woods. At times he hunted on horseback and at other times afoot.

One early morning, Aurora, the dawn, saw him and became

infatuated by his beauty. Despite her marriage to Tithonus, she took on lovers at will. Since Tithonus was a decrepit old man, her flings brought no rebukes.

The dawn was particularly beautiful that morning and Aurora's infatuation was returned by her chosen lover.

Leaving his dog and, when mounted, his horse, to wander free, Cephalus lay outstretched on the turf and allowed dawn's rosy fingers to have their way with his naked body, caressing his dick.

One morning, Procris, full of jealousy and suspicion, awoke before her husband, feigned sleep, and when he left the cottage, stealthily followed him.

Just before dawn, she spied him lying spread-eagle on the forest floor. When dawn broke in the East, she observed her husband's pecker turn into a hardon. Then, after he shuddered in obvious delight, she was amazed to see him ejaculate into the air.

When dawn had progressed into daylight, Cephalus arose.

Procris came out of her hiding place. She demanded that her husband not lie on the ground at dawn any more. Both of them were aware that the demand was not a rational or a reasonable one, but he could not think of any reason to refuse.

Aurora was not devastated. She had recently caught sight of Orion, who was considerably huskier than Cephalus and thus gave more area for her rosy-fingered attentions.

Although he missed Aurora's sweet ministrations, Cephalus' enthusiasm for the hunt was not diminished. He was still up before dawn and was ranging through woods, over hill and across rill. He ignored Aurora's approach as she ignored his previously irresistible physique.

After avid pursuit of game, when the sun had risen to its zenith, Cephalus sought a shady nook bordered by a bubbling brook. He stretched out his fatigued body on the inviting grass in anticipation of the warm caress of a cool breeze.

Zephyrus, the friendly west wind, was aware of Cephalus' availability. He arrived and literally responded to the hunter's fantasy. For Zephyrus enjoys nothing more than caressing the bodies of mortals.

The west wind began by grazing the youth's face and neck,

causing delightful tingles to course up and down his spine.

Cephalus responded with a relaxed sigh and whispered, "Ah, sweet zephyr. Welcome."

The invitation was clear enough to Zephyrus who breathed into the youth's hair that flowed from his scalp, then ruffled his pubic hairs, and subsequently gave a sweet caress to the downy hair that graced his masculine body.

The effect on the hunter was wildly priapic.

The sensation was quite different from the endearments he had received from Aurora. After all, Zephyrus is male, thus differing from the female dawn's rosy fingered fondling. In his younger days Cephalus had engaged in fondling sessions with youths who were his own age. When his interest had turned to girls, he was profoundly aware of how delightfully gentler their touch was to his genitalia. Not that one form of fondling was preferable. Other than that with the girls the practice led to further delights unimaginable with males.

Zephyrus' embraces, like Aurora's, always led to orgasm. And as the west wind's osculation drew the young man's responses to a crescendo, Cephalus, in a kind of euphoric delirium, muttered loving words to his airy afternoon companion.

But hark! Although far from habitation, an inquisitive wanderer happened to pass by at a distance. The gossipy wanderer overheard Cephalus, who was apparently addressing someone with rapturous cooing.

The tattling trespasser recognized Cephalus' voice and beat a hasty path to Procris' cottage to rat on her husband.

Procris, again suspicious and jealous, was willing to believe the informer's tale and in anger hastened to find her husband.

When she arrived at the bucolic spot where Cephalus was sprawled was enjoying Zephyr's twiddling breath on his dong, she was prepared to rant. But, seeing he was unaccompanied, as he had been previously when she had barged upon him at dawn, she was perplexed.

On this occasion, Cephalus did not retreat into an abandonment of his unseen benefactor.

In gentle tones he bade his spouse disrobe and lie next to him. She succumbed to his request.

Zephyrus is, as we all know, omnisexual. He happily caresses every and all of Nature's creatures, male, female, human, animal, and divine. The pleasure of the kiss of the west wind is ubiquitous and all-embracing.

Stretched out beside her husband in exuberant nudity, Procris gave herself over to Zephyrus' soft promiscuity. She succumbed to the pleasure of the soft breeze playing over her cunt. But, unlike Cephalus, she had three or more orgasms to his one.

Thenceforth, throughout the couple's life, Zephyrus called Procris from her cottage on occasion, whence she went to seek her husband. And, together, hand in hand, they enjoyed the thrill of Nature's windfuck.

CHAPTER XXXI

GLAUCUS SHAGS A MERMAID

The goddess Cybele, the Great Earth Mother, endowed every woman on earth with the ability to experience perfect, cataclysmic, overpowering sexual satisfaction every time she engages in sex. Every woman is born with the Goddess embodied within her. The Goddess need only be awakened for the Great Cosmic Orgasm to erupt within her.

Cybele, however, is a somewhat quirky goddess. Consequently she placed a stipulation on the experience of her great erotic gift. Not every man on earth was blessed with the ability to awaken the goddess within womankind, enabling the perfectly satisfying orgasm. Not at all. The gift to the male species is quite frugally dispensed by the Great Mother.

Most men, in a remote corner of their souls, are aware that they do not possess the ability to completely satisfy the women in their lives. But male ego does not allow them to admit this to themselves and most certainly not to others.

Most women hide their dissatisfaction with their lovers' puny attempts at lovemaking but their motherly instincts impel them to attempt to assure their mates that they have succeeded in satisfying them.

Cybele looked down on her domain one day and capriciously granted her boon to a poor fisherman by the name of Glaucus.

Glaucus was not particularly favored in countenance or physique. Nor was there anything notable about his lovemaking equipment. His dick would not be considered long, short, thick, or slim. Size had nothing to do with his ability to satisfy his conquests.

Nor was he endowed with a wart on his peckerhead, a feature prized by those who possessed the bump.

Nor was there any technique in the ars amatoria in which Glaucus excelled. His foreplay activities could not be considered more than adequate.

But when he made love to a woman, the goddess within her warmed, glowed, flourished, and the deep female sexuality that is always ready to burst into flame was ignited.

One could say that the Great Mother Goddess had rewarded the fisherman lavishly. But the reward was not earned in any way. It was given on whim alone.

Glaucus had known and satisfied many women. He had not seen fit to promise the marriage couch to any one.

One day, as he stood by a river emptying his nets and sorting his catch, the entire lot propelled itself by use of its fins to return to the water and swim away.

Glaucus observed the scene with wonder. What could cause such an unexpected happening? Could it be the strange plants that grew among the herbage upon which he had discharged his nets?

Glaucus had never been aware before of the herbs that had sprung up in the grassy patch beneath his feet. He stooped down and plucked a sprout. He sniffed at the herb. Hmmm. *Aromatic. What do you suppose this tastes like?*

The fisherman took a bite, and as the juices were ingested, he felt strongly impelled to follow the path his catch had created into the water. For the herb was Ptythis, a rare plant that enchants those who partake of it.

He went to the river's edge and with an exuberant shout dove into the inviting waters.

He was welcomed by the water nymphs, the oceanides, who had been informed by the water demigods of Glaucus' gift. They were all anxious to experience the erotic rapture that the more fortunate landlubber women had been favored with.

The water nymphs led Glaucus to their parents, Oceanus and Tethys, the sovereigns of the sea. Glaucus could think of nothing more attractive than to have access to the beautiful creatures that inhabited the water and requested to be admitted to their fold.

They welcomed him immediately into their company, whereupon he found that his hair, that flowed gorgeously behind him, had turned green, his shoulders had broadened, his thighs and his legs melded into the form of a fish's tail. He had, in short, become a merman. And, like the others of his kind, he was graced with a penis at the location where he previously had a crotch.

Oh what a time Glaucus had. He had his choice of all the mermaids. Mortals who encountered mermaids were unable to discern their snatches. Not so Glaucus, who had become a demigod. The smoothness of his scaly lower body when pressed against that of the mermaids as he penetrated their cunts, if anything, brought on even higher degree or orgasm to the sea-lovely than to her counterpart who trod the earth.

He entered naiads and oceanides from within their welcoming spread legs. In short, his range of female companionship was increased by his newly acquired state a hundredfold.

Of course, he was now amphibious and could slither ashore to make love to the river nymphs who dwelt on land.

One day he slithered ashore and caught sight of a gorgeous water-nymph named Scylla. He fell madly in love with her at first sight.

He attempted to tell her that he was one of those blessed by Cybele with the power to make exquisite love.

Scylla ran away, ascending a knoll and turned back to observe what kind of creature had emerged from the water.

Glaucus attempted to urge her back to the shore by elaborating on his priapic endowment. But Scylla would have nothing to do with his pleas and ran off to dangle her feet in a distant pond where she could not be pursued by the merman.

Glaucus could not get over his love-struck state and decided to consult the famous sorceress Circe.

He swam to her island and flopped his way to her cave.

He ignored all the pigs that were rooting around and addressed her beseechingly.

"O widely renowned sorceress. I come to you for your succor. Recently I emerged from the sea and caught sight of a beautiful water-nymph named Scylla. I am madly in love with her. But she is deaf to my protestations of love, even though I try to explain to her that I am a creature endowed with the Gift of Cybele."

Circe was, indeed, a great sorceress. She was a very randy sorceress as a matter fact. But with all her magical abilities she had never been able to attract one of Cybele's beneficiaries. There was nothing on land or in the sea that she desired more than to experience the Grand Orgasm. And here, right in her cave, was the creature of her dreams. And the merman appeared to her to be particularly attractive with his green hair, his broad shoulders, and the boner that was arising from his midsection under her seductive ogling.

"You are too good for that slut of a naiad," she replied. "What you need is a female who can appreciate what you've got there. Someone who can show you a real hot time in exchange for that gift you have."

Glaucus, of course, got the point. And he found Circe to be a very sexy enchantress. But he still wanted Scylla to succumb to him.

Circe agreed to help him if he would consent to make love to her.

Glaucus was hardly averse to the idea. He was about to agree when one of the pigs that swarmed about the place caught his attention and gave him a warning.

"Listen to me, Merman," quoth the pig. "Look around you. All of us swine here were once men. We sailed the seas brave and free. We were lured to this cave, one by one, by the evil sorceress who is propositioning you. She welcomed each of us to a merry romp between her legs. And she's good. Real good. She can keep you on the edge for an hour or more. But as soon as you come and withdraw, she turns you into a pig. Ain't that so, lads?"

All the swine nodded their heads in agreement.

Circe patiently allowed the pig his say and then kicked him rudely aside.

"The swine speaks sooth," she told her guest. "Each of these animal swine was once a human swine whose male ego made him think he could satisfy every living woman. I gave them their chance, and when each had blown his wad, I gave him his just deserts.

"It will not be that way with you, my pretty. In the first place, that particular sorcery works only on mortals. You are a demigod and thus immune. But more compelling yet is your gift from the Great Mother Goddess. There is not a female creature on land or in the sea who can possibly be disappointed by your lovemaking. Come, beautiful merman. Shag me here and now and I promise to do my best to win your nymph for you if that is really what you desire. I only ask that you return to me afterwards."

"I cannot really perform with all these pigs around," Glaucus responded. "Please restore them to their former state and send them on their way."

"Gladly," the witch agreed.

She wove an incantation. The swine were transformed to human form and practically trampled each other to death to get out of the cave and out onto the seashore.

With the cave empty but for the remaining lovers, Circe took her merman lover to her seaweed couch and into her yearning arms.

Of course Circe was satisfied. Cybele's gift never failed. But Glaucus was also carried to ecstasies he had not previously even imagined by the enchantress' skillful vaginal maneuvering.

True to her promise, Circe sent Glaucus to Sicily, where she knew Scylla had repaired. The merman had with him an amulet that, when seen by any nymph, would draw her to him.

He swam to the island and emerged at the shore where Scylla was dangling her lovely legs in the choppy waves.

Glaucus flashed the amulet at the nymph. When she saw it she was, indeed, drawn towards the merman. But she was in an ill mood and shouted all the fowl curses she had learned from the sailors she had met.

Upon hearing the vile imprecations issuing from the nymph's lips, Glaucus fell out of love and withdrew the amulet from her sight.

Glaucus swam back to Circe's island and back into her arms.

They dwelt together in perfect harmony. Circe allowed him to abandon the cave as often as he wished in search of females to pleasure – females who dwelt on land or under water.

While he was absent, Circe did not lack for lovers. And she was not above practicing a bit of evil magic on the seafarers who were attracted to her cave. On one occasion she entertained Ulysses and his crew on their way back home from Troy. Homer relates that adventure in stunningly beautiful dactylic hexameters.

But when Glaucus is back with her in her cave, where their mutual embraces are exuberantly blissful, Circe is possibly the best behaved enchantress below Mount Olympus.

ABOUT THE AUTHOR

TIM DESMONDES

Tim Desmondes was born and raised in Los Angeles. He has lived his entire life in California and has resided in many communities in that state.

Tim currently lives with his wife in a beach town in Southern California.

Tim is also the author of:

Sex and Loathing in Hollywood

Sexual Diversity and Perversity

Dracula Sucks Hollywood Dudes

Venus Does Adonis while Apollo Shags a Tree

*Available at Amazon.com, TheNazcaPlainsCorp.com
and your Local Bookstore*